FISHING FOR LAUGHS

A GREAT CATCH OF
FUNNY FISHING TALES

BY

VARIOUS AUTHORS

British Library Cataloguing-in-Publication Data
A catalogue record for this book is available from the
British Library

CONTENTS

TWADDLE ON TWEEDSIDE

Christopher North

TWADDLE ON TWEEDSIDE

Angling, in boyhood, youth, and manhood's prime, was with us a passion. Now it is an affection. The first glimpse of the water, caught at a distance, used to set our hearts a-beating, and 'Without stop or stay down the rocky way' we rushed to the pastime.

If we saw a villain with a creel on his back, wading waist-deep, and from the middle of the stream commanding every cranny in among the tree roots on both sides – in spite of copse or timber – we cursed and could almost have killed him; and how we guffawed when such a reprobate, at a chance time losing his footing among the coggly and sliddery stones, with many staggers, fell sprawling first back and then forwards, and finally, half-choked and grievously incommoded by the belt of his emptied basket coiling round his thrapple, while the dead trouts were seen floating about with their yellow bellies, went hatless down the current, and came sneaking out at the ford like a half-drowned rat – pity that the vagabond had not gone over the waterfall – a better death than his father's, who, it was well known, was hanged for sheep-stealing at Carlisle!

Now we can look carelessly at a whole regiment of leathern-aprons, all at once in single file poaching the Tweed the whole way from Peebles to Innerleithen. Nothing that may happen in this world now would make us lose our temper. With the utmost equanimity we can now look up to our tailfly – both bobbers – and several yards of line, inextricably hanked, high up a tree; or on the whole concern by a sudden jerk converted into an extraordinary hair-ball, such as one reads of being found in the stomachs of cows. The sudden breaking of our top just at the joint, which is left full of rotten wood – no knife in our pocket and no spare top in our butt – a calamity which has caused frequent suicides – from us elicits but a philosophical smile at the Vanity of Human Wishes.

Here's as pretty a piece of workmanship as the rod maker Phin ever put out of hand – light as cork, and true as steel – and such a run! Now, let us choose an irresistible leash of insects – and we lay a sovereign to a sixpence that we are fast in silver scales before half-a-dozen throws. Where the deuce is our tackle-book? Not in this pocket – nor this – nor this – nor this. Confound it – that is very odd – it can't surely be in our breeches – no – no – not there – curse it – that is very queer – nor in the crown of our hat – no – dang it – that is enough to try the patience of a saint! Where the devil can it be? Not in our basket – no—and Tommy! can we, like an infernal idiot, have left our book on the breakfast table back at Clovenford?

O the born idiots of the Inn! Not to see our book lying on the breakfast table. The blind blockheads must have taken it for the family Bible. And Helen, too! not to see and send it after us! Never again, were we to drag on a miserable existence like Methusaleh's, will we have the wretched folly to come out to Clovenford! From this blasted hour we swear to give up angling for ever – and we have a mind to break into twenty thousand pieces this great, big, thick, coarse, clumsy, useless and lumbering rod!

We beseech us to look at *that – the take – the take is on* – by all that is prolific, the surface of the water is crawling with noses and back-fins – scores of pounders are plumping about in all directions – and oh, Gemini! the ripple over by yonder, in the shallow water of that little greensward-bottomed bay, betrays a monster. Such a day, and such an hour, and such a minute for certain slaughter – for bloody sport – never saw we with our eyes – though we have for fifty years and more been an angler. People in pulpits preach patience – blockheads in black and with bands – smooth and smug smiling sinners who never knew disappointment nor despair – nor have the souls of the poor prigs capacity to conceive such a trial as this. There they go – heads and tails – leap-leap-leaping – but no splash – for the largest dip noiselessly as the least – and we hear only a murmur. – Oh lord!

Why are not people planting potatoes somewhere in sight? Nobody dibbling in the garden. Door of the house locked – but we might walk into the byre. The fools have gone to the fair! We are deafened by eternal talk about education in Scotland – why then is there not here a school – that we might get a boy to run to Clovenford for our book? It seems especially absurd for the county to have put itself to great expense in making a turnpike road through such an uninhabited district as this. Not a soul to be seen far as the

eye can reach – nothing in the live way but sheep and rooks
– and they do bleat and caw, it must be confessed, to an
odious degree, and in a most disgusting manner. As to going
back all the way, two Scotch – but many English miles – to
Clovenford for our book – and then coming back to begin
fishing about the middle of the day – when it is well known
that it often unaccountably happens you may then as well
angle in the Tweed for oysters – that would be madness; yet
staying here without tackle is folly; and in such a dilemma,
what the devil – we say again – is to be done? But who is this
suddenly arrived?

Heaven bless thy bright face, thou golden-headed girl!
whence comest thou into this nook of earth – yes – from
Fairyland. What? Herding cows? Well – well – child! don't
be frightened – you have overheard us talking to ourselves
– and perhaps think us "the strange Gentleman"; but it was
a mere soliloquy – so see – here's half-a-crown – run you to
Cloven-ford and ask Helen for our book – our tackle-book
– and you shall have another on your return – provided you
are back within the hour. Never mind about the cows. We
will look after them – CHRISTOPHER NORTH IN THE
CHARACTER OF COWHERD – what a subject for our
dear Wullie Allan! Yet, did not Apollo for nine years guard
the flocks of Admetus?

Why, 'tis but nine now. Time enough from ten to six to

crowd our creel, till the lid fly open. Many a man would have been much discomposed on such an occasion as this; but thanks to a fine natural temper, and to a philosophic and religious education, we have kept ourselves cool as a cucumber. This forgetfulness of ours is likely to prove a lucky accident after all, for hitherto there has been hardly a breath stirring, and we did not much like that glimmer on the water. True, a few fins were visible – but they were merely playing, and we question if a single snout would have taken the fly. But now the air is beginning to circulate, and to go rustling up among the thick-budded, and here and there almost leafy trees, in little delightful whirlwinds. The sun is sobered in the mild sky by the gentle obscuration of small soft rainy or rather dewy-looking clouds; one feels the inexpressible difference between heat and warmth, in this genial temperature; and what could have been the matter with our eyes that they were blind, or with our soul that it was insensible, to that prodigal profusion of primroses embedding the banks and braes with beauty, in good time to be succeeded by the yet brighter broom!

Shall we take a swim? The cow-herdess might surprise us in the pool, and swoon with fear at sight of the water-kelpie!

A dream of old, born of that sudden smile

Of watery sunshine, comes across our brain.

Twenty years ago, at two o'clock of a summer morning

10

we left the schoolhouse at Dalmally, where we were lodging, and walked up Glenorchy – fourteen miles long – to Inveruren. On the banks of that fishy loch we stood, eyeing the sunshine beautifully warming the breezy dark moss-water. We unscrewed the brass head of our walking cane, to convert it into a rod; when, lo! the hollow was full of emptiness! We had disembowelled it the evening before, and left all the pieces on the chest of drawers in our bedroom! This was as bad as being without our book. The dizziness in our head was as if the earth had dwindled down to the size of the mere spot on which we stood, but still kept moving as before at the same rate, on its own axis, and round the sun. On recovering our stationary equilibrium, we put our pocket pistol to our head, and blew out its brains into our mouth – in the liquid character of Glenlivet. Then down the glen we bounded like a deer belling in his season, and by half past seven were in the schoolhouse. We said nothing – not that we were either sullen or sulky; but stern resolution compressed out lips, which opened but to swallow a few small loaves and fishes – and having performed twenty-eight miles, we started again for the Loch. At eleven – for we took our swing easily and steadily – our five flies were on the water. By sunset we had killed twenty dozen – none above a pound – and by far the greater number about a quarter – but the *tout-ensemble* was imposing – and the weight could not have been short of five stone. We filled both creels (one used for salmon), bag, and pillowslip, and all the pockets about our person – and at first peep of the evening star went our ways again down the glen towards Dalmally. We reached the schoolhouse 'ae wee short hour ayont the twal,' having been on our legs almost all the four-and-twenty hours, and for eight up to the waist in water – distance walked, fifty-six miles – trouts killed, twenty dozen and odds – and weight carried.

At the close of the day when the hamlet was still,

And mortals the sweets of forgetfulness proved,

certainly seventy pounds for fourteen miles; and if the tale be not true, may Mayday miss Maga.

And, now, alas! we could not hobble for our book from the holms of Ashiestiel to Clovenford!

But here comes Iris, with our book in her bosom. She espies us, and holding it up above 'her beautiful and shining golden head,' it seems to our ears as if the kind creature were singing a song.

Now, Mary – we knew your name was Mary, the moment we saw you – Mary Riddle – we ken you sing – sae gie's a sang, my bonny bit wee winsome lassie – while we are rummaging our book. But what's the matter? What's the matter?

'O sir,' she says, 'you've no been leukin after the kye – for, mercy me! there's three o' the twa-year-auld Hielant nowt gotten into the garden. O Sir! you're a bad herd!'

A SHARK STORY

Thomas Chandler Haliburton

A SHARK STORY

'Well, gentlemen, I'll go ahead, if you say so. Here's the story. It is true, upon my honour, from beginning to end – every word of it. I once crossed over to Faulkner's island to fish for *tautaugs*, as the north-side people call black fish, on the reefs hard by, in the Long Island Sound. Tim Titus (who died of the dropsy down at Shinnecock point, last spring) lived there then. Tim was a right good fellow, only he drank rather too much.

'It was during the latter part of July; the sharks and the dog-fish had just begun to spoil sport. When Tim told me about the sharks, I resolved to go prepared to entertain these aquatic savages with all becoming attention and regard, if there should chance to be any interloping about our fishing ground. So, we rigged out a set of extra large hooks, and shipped some rope-yarn and steel chain, an axe, a couple of clubs, and an old harpoon, in addition to our ordinary equipments, and off we started. We threw out our anchor at half ebb tide, and took some thumping large fish; two of them weighed thirteen pounds – so you may judge. The reef where we lay was about half a mile from the island, and, perhaps, a mile from the Connecticut shore. We floated there, very quietly, throwing out and hauling in, until the breaking of my line, with a sudden and severe jerk, informed me that the sea attorneys were in waiting, down stairs; and we accordingly prepared to give them a retainer. A salt pork cloak upon one of our magnum hooks forthwith engaged one of the gentlemen in our service. We got him alongside, and by dint of piercing, and thrusting, and banging, we accomplished a most exciting and merry murder. We had business enough of the kind to keep us employed until near low water. By this time, the sharks had all cleared out, and the black fish were biting again; the rock began to make its appearance above the water, and in a little while its hard bald head was entirely dry. Tim now proposed to set me out upon the rock, while he rowed ashore to get the jug, which, strange to say, we had left at the house. I assented to this proposition; first, because I began to feel the effects of the sun upon my tongue, and needed something to take, by the way of medicine; and secondly because the rock was a favourite spot for rod and reel, and famous for luck: so I took my *traps*, and a box of bait, and jumped upon my new station. Tim made for the island.

'Not many men would willingly have been left upon a little barren reef that was covered by every flow of the tide, in the midst of a waste of waters, at such a distance from the shore, even with an assurance from a companion more to be depended upon than mine, that he would return immediately and take him off. But some how or other, the excitement of the sport was so high, and the romance of the situation was so delightful, that I thought of nothing else but the prospect of my fun, and the contemplation of the novelty and beauty of the scene. It was a mild, pleasant afternoon, in harvest time. The sky was clear and pure. The deep blue sound, heaving all around me, was studded with craft of all descriptions and dimensions, from the dipping sail-boat to the rolling merchantman, sinking and rising like sea-birds sporting with their white wings in the surge. The grain and grass on the neighbouring farms were gold and green, and gracefully they bent obeisance to a gently breathing southwester. Farther off, the high upland, and the distant coast, gave a dim relief to the prominent features of the landscape, and seemed the rich but dusky frame of a brilliant fairy picture. Then, how still it was! Not a sound could be heard, except the occasional rustling of my own motion, and the water beating against the sides, or gurgling in the fissures of the rock, or except now and then the cry of a solitary saucy gull, who would come out of his way in the firmament, to see what I was doing without a boat, all alone, in the middle of the sound; and who would hover, and cry, and chatter, and make two or three circling swoops and dashes at me, and then, after having satisfied his curiosity, glide away in search of some other food to scream at.

'I soon became half indolent, and quite indifferent about fishing; so I stretched myself out at full length upon the rock and gave myself up to the luxury of looking and thinking. The divine exercise soon put me fast asleep. I dreamed away a couple of hours, and longer might have dreamed, but for a tired fish-hawk who chose to make my head his resting place, and who waked and started me to my feet.

' "Where is Tim Titus?" I muttered to myself, as I strained my eyes over the now darkened water. But none was near me to answer that interesting question, and nothing was to be seen of either Tim or his boat. "He should have been here long ere this," thought I, "and he promised faithfully not to stay long – could he have forgotten? or has he paid too much devotion to the jug?"

'I began to feel uneasy, for the tide was rising fast, and soon would cover the top of the rock, and high water mark was at least a foot above my head. I buttoned up my coat, for either the coming coolness of the evening, or else my growing apprehensions, had set me trembling and chattering most painfully. I braced my nerves, and set my teeth, and tried to hum "Begone, dull care," keeping time with my fists upon my thighs. But what music! What melancholy merriment! I started and shuddered at the doleful sound of my own voice. I am not naturally a coward; but I should like to know the man who would not, in such a situation, be alarmed. It is a cruel death to die to be merely drowned, and to go through the ordinary commonplaces of suffocation; but to see your death gradually rising to your eyes, to feel the water rising, inch by inch, upon your shivering sides, and to anticipate the certainly coming, choking struggle for your last breath, when, with the gurgling sound of an overflowing brook taking a new direction, the cold brine pours into mouth, ears, and nostrils, usurping the seat and avenues of health and life, and, with gradual flow, stifling –

smothering – suffocating! It were better to die a thousand common deaths.

'This is one of the instances in which, it must be admitted, salt water is not a pleasant subject of contemplation. However, the rock was not yet covered, and hope, blessed hope, stuck faithfully by me. To beguile, if possible, the weary time, I put on a bait, and threw out for fish. I was sooner successful than I could have wished to be, for hardly had my line struck the water, before the hook was swallowed, and my rod was bent with the dead hard pull of a twelve foot shark. I let him run about fifty yards, and then reeled up. He appeared not at all alarmed, and I could scarcely feel him bear upon my fine hair line. He followed the pull gently and unresisting, came up to the rock, laid his nose upon its side, and looked up into my face, not as if utterly unconcerned, but with a sort of quizzical impudence, as though he perfectly understood the precarious nature of my situation. The conduct of my captive renewed and increased my alarm. And well it might; for the tide was now running over a corner of the rock behind me, and a small stream rushed through a cleft, or fissure, by my side, and formed a puddle at my very feet. I broke my hook out of the monster's mouth, and leaned upon my rod for support.

' "Where is Tim Titus?" I cried aloud. "Curse on the drunken vagabond! Will he never come?"

'My ejaculations did no good. No Timothy appeared. It became evident that I must prepare for drowning, or for action. The reef was completely covered, and the water was above the soles of my feet. I was not much of a swimmer, and as to ever reaching the island, I could not even hope for that. However, there was no alternative, and I tried to encourage myself, by reflecting that necessity was the mother of invention, and that desperation will sometimes ensure success. Besides, too, I considered and took comfort from the thought that I could wait for Tim, so long as I had a foothold, and then commit myself to the uncertain strength of my arms and legs for salvation. So I turned my bait-box upside down, and mounting upon that, endeavoured to comfort my spirits, and to be courageous, but submissive to my fate. I thought of death, and what it might bring with it, and I tried to repent of the multiplied iniquities of my almost wasted life; but I found that that was no place for a sinner to settle his accounts. Wretched soul, pray I could not.

'The water had not got above my ankles, when, to my inexpressible joy, I saw a sloop bending down towards me, with the evident intention of picking me up. No man can imagine what were the sensations of gratitude which filled my bosom at that moment.

'When she got within a hundred yards of the reef, I

sung out to the man at the helm to luff up, and lie by, and lower the boat; but to my amazement, I could get no reply, nor notice of my request. I entreated them, for the love of heaven, to take me off; and I promised, I know not what rewards, that were entirely beyond my power of bestowal. But the brutal wretch of a captain, muttering something to the effect of "that he hadn't time to stop," and giving me the kind and sensible advice to pull off my coat and swim ashore, put the helm hard down, and away bore the sloop on the other tack.

' "Heartless villain!" I shrieked out, in the torture of my disappointment; "may God reward your inhumanity."

'The crew answered my prayer with a coarse, loud laugh; and the cook asked me through a speaking trumpet, "If I was not afraid of catching cold." – The black rascal!

'It now was time to strip; for my knees felt the cool tide, and the wind dying away, left a heavy swell, that swayed and shook the box upon which I was mounted, so that I had occasionally to stoop, and paddle with my hands against the water in order to preserve my perpendicular. The setting sun sent his almost horizontal streams of fire across the dark waters, making them gloomy and terrific, by the contrast of his amber and purple glories.

'Something glided by me in the water, and then made a sudden halt. I looked upon the black mass, and, as my eye ran along its dark outline, I saw, with horror, that it was a shark; the identical monster out of whose mouth I had just broken my hook. He was fishing now for me, and was evidently only waiting for the tide to rise high enough above the rock, to glut at once his hunger and revenge. As the water continued to mount above my knees, he seemed to grow more hungry and familiar. At last, he made a desperate dash, and approaching within an inch of my legs, turned upon his back, and opened his huge jaws for an attack. With desperate strength, I thrust the end of my rod violently at his mouth; and the brass head, ringing against his teeth, threw him back into the deep current, and I lost sight of him entirely. This, however, was but a momentary repulse; for in the next minute he was close behind my back, and pulling at the skirts of my fustian coat, which hung dipping into the water. I leaned forward hastily, and endeavoured to extricate myself from the dangerous grasp; but the monster's teeth were too firmly set, and his immense strength nearly drew me over. So, down flew my rod, and off went my jacket, devoted peace offerings to my voracious visitor.

'In an instant, the waves all round me were lashed into froth and foam. No sooner was my poor old sporting friend drawn under the surface, than it was fought for by at least a dozen enormous combatants! The battle raged upon every side. High black fins rushed now here, now there, and long, strong tails scattered sleet and froth, and the brine was thrown up in jets, and eddied and curled, and fell, and swelled, like a whirlpool in Hell-gate.

'Of no long duration, however, was this fishy tourney. It seemed soon to be discovered that the prize contended for contained nothing edible but cheese and crackers, and no flesh; and as its mutilated fragments rose to the surface, the waves subsided into their former smooth condition. Not till then did I experience the real terrors of my situation. As I looked around me to see what had become of the robbers, I counted one, two, three, yes, up to twelve, successively, of the largest sharks I ever saw, floating in a circle around me, like divergent rays, all mathematically equidistant from the rock, and from each other; each perfectly motionless, and with his gloating, fiery eye, fixed full and fierce upon me. Basilisks and rattlesnakes! how the fire of their steady eyes entered into my heart! I was the centre of a circle, whose radii were sharks! I was the unsprung, or rather *unchewed* game, at which a pack of hunting sea-dogs were making a dead point!

'There was one old fellow, that kept within the circumference of the circle. He seemed to be a sort of captain, or leader of the band; or, rather, he acted as the coroner for the other twelve of the inquisition, that were summoned to sit on, and eat up my body. He glided around and about, and every now and then would stop, and touch his nose against some one of his comrades, and seem to consult, or to give instructions as to the time and mode of operation. Occasionally, he would skull himself up towards me, and examine the condition of my flesh, and then again glide back, and rejoin the troupe, and flap his tail, and have another confabulation. The old rascal had, no doubt, been out into the highways and byways, and collected this company of his friends and kinfish, and invited them to supper.

'I must confess, that horribly as I felt, I could not help but think of a tea party, of demure old maids, sitting in a solemn circle, with their skinny hands in their laps, licking their expectant lips, while their hostess bustles about in the important functions of her preparations. With what an eye have I seen such appurtenances of humanity survey the location and adjustment of some especial condiment, which is about to be submitted to criticism and consumption.

'My sensations began to be, now, most exquisite indeed; but I will not attempt to describe them. I was neither hot nor cold, frightened nor composed; but I had a combination of all kinds of feelings and emotions. The present, past, future, heaven, earth, my father and mother, a little girl I knew once, and the sharks, were all confusedly mixed up together, and swelled my crazy brain almost to bursting. I cried, and laughed, and spouted, and screamed for Tim Titus.

'In a fit of most wise madness, I opened my broad-bladed fishing knife, and waved it around my head with an air of defiance. As the tide continued to rise, my extravagance of madness mounted. At one time, I became persuaded that my tide-waiters were reasonable beings, who might be talked into mercy and humanity, if a body could only hit upon the right text. So, I bowed, and gesticulated, and threw out my hands, and talked to them, as friends, and brothers, members of my family, cousins, uncles, aunts, people waiting to have their bills paid; I scolded them as my servants; I abused them as duns; I implored them as jurymen sitting on the question of my life; I congratulated, and flattered them as my comrades upon some glorious enterprise; I sung and ranted to them, now as an actor in a play-house, and now as an elder at a camp-meeting; in one moment, roaring,

On this cold flinty rock I will lay down my head,—

and in the next, giving out to my attentive hearers for singing, a hymn of Dr. Watts so admirably appropriate to the occasion:

On slippery rocks I see them stand,

While fiery billows roll below.

'What said I, what did I not say! Prose and poetry, scripture and drama, romance and ratiocination – out it came. "*Quamdiu, Catalina, nostra patientia abutere?*" – I sung out to the old captain, to begin with: "My brave associates, partners of my toil," – so ran the strain. "On which side soever I turn my eyes," – "Gentlemen of the jury," – "I come not here to steal away your hearts," – "You are not wood, you are not stones, but" – "Hah!" – "Begin, ye tormentors, your tortures are vain," – "Good friends, sweet friends, let me not stir you up to any sudden flood," – "The angry flood that lashed her groaning sides," – "Ladies and gentlemen," – "My very noble and approved good masters," – "Avaunt! and quit my sight; let the earth hide ye," – "Lie lightly on his head, O earth!" – "O, heaven and earth, that it should come to this!" – "The torrent roared, and we did buffet it with lusty sinews, stemming it aside and oaring it with hearts of controversy," – "Give me some drink, Titinius," – "Drink, boys, drink, and drown dull sorrow," – "For liquor it doth roll such comfort to the soul," – "Romans, countrymen and lovers, hear me for my cause, and be silent that you may hear," – "Fellow citizens, assembled as we are upon this interesting occasion, impressed with the truth and beauty," – "Isle of beauty, fare thee well," – "The quality of mercy is not strained," – "*Magna veritas et prevalebit,*" – "Truth is potent, and" – "Most potent, grave, and reverend seigniors,"—

Oh, now you weep, and I perceive you feel
The dint of pity; these are gracious drops.
Kind souls! what! weep you when you but behold
Our Caesar's vesture wounded,—

Ha! ha! ha! – and I broke out in a fit of most horrible laughter, as I thought of the mincemeat particles of my lacerated jacket.

'In the meantime, the water had got well up towards my shoulders, and while I was shaking and vibrating upon my uncertain foot-hold, I felt the cold nose of the captain of the band snubbing against my side. Desperately, and without a definite object, I struck my knife at one of his eyes, and, by some singular fortune, cut it out clean from the socket. The shark darted back, and halted. In an instant, hope and reason came to my relief; and it occurred to me, that if I could only blind the monster, I might yet escape. Accordingly, I stood ready for the next attack. The loss of an eye did not seem to affect him much, for after shaking his head once or twice, he came up to me again, and when he was about half an inch off, turned upon his back. This was the critical moment. With a most unaccountable presence of mind, I laid hold of his nose with my left hand, and with my right scooped out his remaining organ of vision. He opened his big mouth, and champed his long teeth at me, in despair. But it was all over with him. I raised my right foot and gave him a hard shove, and he glided off into deep water, and went to the bottom.

'Well, gentlemen, I suppose you'd think it a hard story, but it's none the less a fact, that I served every remaining one

27

of those nineteen sharks in the same fashion. They all came up to me, one by one, regularly and in order, and I scooped their eyes out, and gave them a shove, and they went off into deep water, just like so many lambs. By the time I had scooped out and blinded a couple of dozen of them, they began to seem so scarce that I thought I would swim for the island, and fight the rest for fun, on the way; but just then, Tim Titus hove in sight, and it had got to be almost dark, and I concluded to get aboard and rest myself.'

THE MONSTROUS TROUT

Jerome K. Jerome

THE MONSTROUS TROUT

We stayed two days at Streatley, and got our clothes washed. We had tried washing them ourselves, in the river, under George's superintendence, and it had been a failure. Indeed, it had been more than a failure, because we were worse off after we had washed our clothes than we were before. Before we had washed them, they had been very, very dirty, it is true; but they were just wearable. *After* we had washed them – well, the river between Reading and Henley was much cleaner, after we had washed our clothes in it, than it was before. All the dirt contained in the river between Reading and Henley we collected, during that wash, and worked it into our clothes.

The washerwoman at Streatley said she felt she owed it to herself to charge us just three times the usual prices for that wash. She said it had not been like washing, it had been more in the nature of excavating.

We paid the bill without a murmur.

The neighbourhood of Streatley and Goring is a great fishing centre. There is some excellent fishing to be had here. The river abounds in pike, roach, dace, gudgeon, and eels, just here; and you can sit and fish for them all day.

Some people do. They never catch them. I never knew anybody catch anything up the Thames, except minnows and dead cats, but that has nothing to do, of course, with fishing! The local fisherman's guide doesn't say a word about catching anything. All it says is the place is 'a good station for fishing'; and from what I have seen of the district, I am quite prepared to bear out this statement.

There is no spot in the world where you can get more fishing, or where you can fish for a longer period. Some fishermen come here and fish for a day, and others stop and fish for a month. You can hang on and fish for a year, if you want to: it will be all the same.

The *Angler's Guide to the Thames* says that 'jack and perch are also to be had about here,' but there the *Angler's Guide* is wrong. Jack and perch may *be* about there. Indeed, I know for a fact that they are. You can *see* them there in shoals, when you are out for a walk along the banks; they come and stand half out of the water with their mouths open for biscuits. And, if you go for a bathe, they crowd round, and get in your way and irritate you. But they are not to be 'had' by a bit of worm on the end of a hook, nor anything like it – not they!

I am not a good fisherman myself. I devoted a considerable amount of attention to the subject at one time, and was getting on, as I thought, fairly well; but the old hands told me that I should never be any real good at it, and advised me to give it up. They said that I was an extremely neat thrower, and that I seemed to have plenty of gumption for the thing, and quite enough constitutional laziness. But they were sure I should never make anything of a fisherman. I had not got sufficient imagination.

They said that as a poet, or a shilling shocker, or a reporter, or anything of that kind, I might be satisfactory, but that, to gain any position as a Thames angler, would require more play of fancy, more power of invention than I appeared to possess.

Some people are under the impression that all that is

required to make a good fisherman is the ability to tell lies easily and without blushing; but this is a mistake. Mere bald fabrication is useless; the veriest tyro can manage that. It is in the circumstantial detail, the embellishing touches of probability, the general air of scrupulous – almost of pedantic – veracity, that the experienced angler is seen.

Anybody can come in and say, 'Oh, I caught fifteen dozen perch yesterday evening'; or 'Last Monday I landed a gudgeon, weighing eighteen pounds, and measuring three feet from the tip to the tail.'

There is no art, no skill, required for that sort of thing. It shows pluck, but that is all.

No; your accomplished angler would scorn to tell a lie, that way. His method is a study in itself.

He comes in quietly with his hat on, appropriates the most comfortable chair, lights his pipe, and commences to puff in silence. He lets the youngsters brag away for a while, and then, during a momentary lull, he removes the pipe from his mouth, and remarks, as he knocks the ashes out against the bars:

'Well, I had a haul on Tuesday evening that it's not much good my telling anybody about.'

'Oh! why's that?' they ask.

'Because I don't expect anybody would believe me if I did,' replies the old fellow calmly, and without even a tinge of bitterness in his tone, as he refills his pipe, and requests the landlord to bring him three of Scotch, cold.

There is a pause after this, nobody feeling sufficiently sure of himself to contradict the old gentleman. So he has to go on by himself without any encouragement.

'No,' he continues thoughtfully; 'I shouldn't believe it myself if anybody told it to me, but it's a fact, for all that. I had been sitting there all the afternoon and had caught literally nothing – except a few dozen dace and a score of jack; and I was just about giving it up as a bad job when I suddenly felt a rather smart pull at the line. I thought it was another little one, and I went to jerk it up. Hang me, if I could move the rod! It took me half an hour – half an hour, sir! – to land that fish; and every moment I thought the line was going to snap! I reached him at last, and what do you think it was? A sturgeon! a forty pound sturgeon! taken on a line, sir! Yes, you may well look surprised – I'll have another three of Scotch, landlord, please.'

And then he goes on to tell of the astonishment of everybody who saw it; and what his wife said, when he got home, and of what Joe Buggles thought about it.

I asked the landlord of an inn up the river once, if it did not injure him, sometimes, listening to the tales that the fishermen about there told him; and he said:

'Oh, no; not now, sir. It did used to knock me over a bit

at first, but, lor love you! me and the missus we listens to 'em all day now. It's what you're used to, you know. It's what you're used to.'

I knew a young man once, he was a most conscientious fellow and, when he took to fly fishing, he determined never to exaggerate his hauls by more than twenty-five per cent.

'When I have caught forty fish,' said he, 'then I will tell people that I have caught fifty, and so on. But I will not lie any more than that, because it is sinful to lie.'

But the twenty-five per cent. plan did not work well at all. He never was able to use it. The greatest number of fish he ever caught in one day was three, and you can't add twenty-five per cent to three – at least, not in fish.

So he increased his percentage to thirty-three-and-a-third, but that, again, was awkward, when he had only caught one or two; so, to simplify matters, he made up his mind to just double the quantity.

He stuck to this arrangement for a couple of months, and then he grew dissatisfied with it. Nobody believed him when he told them that he only doubled, and he, therefore, gained no credit that way whatever, while his moderation put him at a disadvantage among the other anglers. When he had really caught three small fish, and said he had caught six, it used to make him quite jealous to hear a man, whom he knew for a fact had only caught one, going about telling people he had landed two dozen.

So, eventually he made one final arrangement with himself, which he has religiously held to ever since, and that was to count each fish that he caught as ten, and to assume ten to begin with. For example, if he did not catch any fish at all, then he said he had caught ten fish – you could never catch less than ten fish by his system; that was the foundation of it. Then, if by any chance he really did catch one fish, he called it twenty, while two fish would count thirty, three forty, and so on.

It is a simple and easily worked plan, and there has been some talk lately of its being made use of by the angling fraternity in general. Indeed, the Committee of the Thames Anglers' Association did recommend its adoption about two years ago, but some of the older members opposed it. They said they would consider the idea if the number were doubled, and each fish counted as twenty.

If ever you have an evening to spare, up the river, I should advise you to drop into one of the little village inns, and take a seat in the tap-room. You will be nearly sure to meet one or two old rod-men, sipping their toddy there, and they will tell you enough fishy stories in half an hour to give you indigestion for a month.

George and I – I don't know what had become of Harris; he had gone out and had a shave, early in the afternoon, and had then come back and spent full forty minutes in pipe-claying his shoes, we had not seen him since – George and I, therefore, and the dog, left to ourselves, went for a walk to Wallingford on the second evening, and coming home, we called in at a little riverside inn, for a rest, and other things.

We went into the parlour and sat down. There was an old fellow there, smoking a long clay pipe, and we naturally began chatting.

He told us that it had been a fine day today and we told him that it had been a fine day yesterday, and then we all told each other that we thought it would be a fine day tomorrow; and George said the crops seemed to be coming up nicely.

After that it came out, somehow or other, that we were strangers in the neighbourhood, and that we were going away the next morning.

Then a pause ensued in the conversation, during which our eyes wandered round the room. They finally rested upon a dusty old glass-case, fixed very high up above the chimney-piece, and containing a trout. It rather fascinated me, that trout; it was such a monstrous fish. In fact, at first glance, I thought it was a cod.

'Ah!' said the old gentleman, following the direction of my gaze, 'fine fellow that, ain't he?'

'Quite uncommon,' I murmured; and George asked the old man how much he thought it weighed.

'Eighteen pounds six ounces,' said our friend, rising and taking down his coat. 'Yes,' he continued, 'it wur sixteen year ago, come the third o' next month, that I landed him. I caught him just below the bridge with a minnow. They told me he wur in the river, and I said I'd have him, and so I did. You don't see many fish that size about here now, I'm thinking. Good night, gentlemen, good night.'

And out he went, and left us alone.

We could not take our eyes off the fish after that. It really was a remarkably fine fish. We were still looking at it, when the local carrier, who had just stopped at the inn, came to the door of the room with a pot of beer in his hand, and he also looked at the fish.

'Good-sized trout, that,' said George, turning round to him.

'Ah! you may well say that, sir,' replied the man; and then, after a pull at his beer, he added, 'Maybe you wasn't here, sir, when that fish was caught?'

'No,' we told him. We were strangers in the neighbourhood.

'Ah!' said the carrier, 'then, of course, how should you? It was nearly five years ago that I caught that trout.'

'Oh! was it you who caught it, then?' said I.

'Yes, sir,' replied the genial old fellow. 'I caught him just below the lock – leastways, what was the lock then – one

Friday afternoon; and the remarkable thing about it is that I caught him with a fly. I'd gone out pike fishing, bless you, never thinking of a trout, and when I saw that whopper on the end of my line, blest if it didn't quite take me aback. Well, you see, he weighed twenty-six pound. Good night, gentlemen, good night.'

Five minutes afterwards a third man came in, and described how *he* had caught it early one morning, with bleak; and then he left, and stolid, solemn-looking, middle-aged individual came in, and sat down over by the window.

None of us spoke for a while; but, at length, George turned to the newcomer, and said:

'I beg your pardon, I hope you will forgive the liberty that we – perfect strangers in the neighbourhood – are taking, but my friend here and myself would be so much obliged if you would tell us how you caught that trout up there.'

'Why, who told you I caught the trout?' was the surprised query.

We said that nobody had told us so, but somehow or other we felt instinctively that it was he who had done it.

'Well, it's a most remarkable thing – most remarkable,' answered the stolid stranger, laughing; 'because, as a matter of fact, you are quite right. I did catch it. But fancy your guessing it like that. Dear me, it's really a most remarkable thing.'

And then he went on, and told us how it had taken him half an hour to land it, and how it had broken his rod. He said he had weighed it carefully when he reached home, and it had turned the scale at thirty-four pounds.

He went in his turn, and when he was gone, the landlord came in to us. We told him the various histories we had heard about his trout, and he was immensely amused, and we all laughed very heartily.

'Fancy Jim Bates and Joe Muggles and Mr. Jones and old Billy Maunders all telling you that they had caught it. Ha! ha! ha! Well, that is good,' said the honest old fellow, laughing heartily. 'Yes, they are the sort to give it *me*, to put up in *my* parlour, if *they* had caught it, they are! Ha! ha! ha!'

And then he told us the real history of the fish. It seemed that he had caught it himself, years ago, when he was quite a lad; not by any art or skill, but by that unaccountable luck that appears to always wait upon a boy when he plays the wag from school, and goes out fishing on a sunny afternoon, with a bit of string tied on to the end of a tree.

He said that bringing home that trout had saved him from a whacking, and that even his schoolmaster had said it was worth the rule-of-three and practice put together.

He was called out of the room at his point, and George and I again turned our gaze upon the fish.

It really was a most astonishing trout. The more we looked

at it, the more we marvelled at it.

It excited George so much that he climbed up on the back of a chair to get a better view of it.

And then the chair slipped, and George clutched wildly at the trout-case to save himself, and down it came with a crash, George and the chair on top of it.

'You haven't injured the fish, have you?' I cried in alarm, rushing up.

'I hope not,' said George, rising cautiously and looking about.

But he had. That trout lay shattered into a thousand fragments – I say a thousand, but they may have only been nine hundred. I did not count them.

We thought it strange and unaccountable that a stuffed trout should break up into little pieces like that.

And so it would have been strange and unaccountable, if it had been a stuffed trout, but it was not.

That trout was plaster of Paris.

A CATCH ON THE LINE

by R. Andom

A CATCH ON THE LINE

We wanted to do something, and we thought we would go fishing. We didn't know much about fishing, it is true; but, as Murray somewhat offensively remarked, any fool could sit on the bank and hold a bit of stick over the water.

Wilks said we'd go to Broxbourne. The River Lea is

there – a bit of it – he told us, and fishes; and he knew it was a splendid place for catching things. A fellow of his acquaintance once moved out there with his family, and they hadn't been in the place three weeks before they all caught the scarlatina, and the last time he himself was there he caught a magnificent cold. This sounded alluring, and we agreed to go to Broxbourne and see what *our* luck would be.

Our train, which left Liverpool Street about three, was one of the things that we didn't catch; but there was so much that we did that we could afford to pass that by. To begin with, we caught a most awful wigging from the railway authorities. It sprang in the first instance from an aggrieved porter, who was a victim to Murray's passion for picking up odd fragments of natural laws and illustrating them. While waiting about the platform for the next train, which gave three-quarters of an hour for the proverbial utilisation of idle hands, he illustrated centrifugal force for us with the can of ground-bait we had thoughtfully provided ourselves with. It was cold oatmeal mush, and had been annexed from Mrs Bloggs' pantry in an old beer can by Wilks, who laboured under the delusion that he was quite sufficiently 'up' in all that pertained to the capture of 'tiddlers' to advise and direct us.

Murray slung the can on an old boot-lace and whirled it over and over, at the same time giving us an elaborate and absolutely untruthful reason for the fact that the contents remained passively within it – the can, I mean, not the reason. Of course, all schoolboys are familiar with the experiment, though they may not be enlightened as to cause – being, in fact, very well satisfied with effect – but it was due to centrifugal force, Murray explained.

As Wilks afterwards tersely remarked, the reason why the can flew off at an angle and smacked an inoffensive porter in the eye, and smothered him with ground-bait, was due chiefly to the fact that the boot-lace was rotten.

It was irritating and somewhat painful, doubtless, but we thought the porter made quite an unnecessary amount of fuss over it. He could see very well that it was a pure accident, and it isn't dignified to lose your temper and storm at a man who has met with misfortune, even though you suffer from the effects of it. Of course wilful aggression is another matter, and there are occasions when the militant attitude is not only advisable, but necessary.

We had quite a large gathering of officials and passengers round us by the time the porter had done expressing his views, and the sympathy was so obviously with him that we advised Murray to try the soothing effect of a bit of silver, and cleared off and allowed him to take it or not as he deemed best. Anyway, we had lost our ground-bait, and, as Wilks remarked, that was as much as we could be expected to contribute.

Wilks made for the refreshment room, Troddles retreated to get a shave, and I hung about the bookstall, and by the time our train came in Murray had settled the matter to everybody's satisfaction, except his own. He said he recognised that we had some sort of claim on him, and his knowledge was always at the service of humanity; but, all the same, he thought half-a-crown was too much to pay to enlighten our insane intellects on the manifold beauties and wonders of centrifugal force.

I told him that he had not paid for enlightening our intellects, but for darkening the porter's eye, and considering what a lovely splash he had had with that ground-bait I considered that it was a cheap lot.

Murray was inclined to argue the matter, so we shoved him into an empty smoker and sat on him until the train ran out of the station.

A little levity does not come amiss, if it is in season and in bounds; but one might almost as well have charge of a pack of schoolboys as to take Wilks and Murray out for an afternoon. Better in fact, because you could clump their heads and reduce them to order, whereas Murray and Wilks are past the clumpable stage, and haven't sufficient balance to justify an appeal to their sense of dignity.

It was a fairly fast train, and was not timed to stop until

we got to Waltham; so Troddles curled himself up in a corner and went to sleep, and I monopolised the other and became absorbed in my pipe and a magazine.

When next I came to a recollection of commonplace, ordinary, everyday affairs, we were speeding through Tottenham Station, and Murray was remarking, 'Come out of it, Wilks. If I had known you were going to stick there all the journey, I'd have taken first go.'

I looked up, and found Wilks with a foot on either seat and his head poked out of the lamp-hole in the roof. It struck me as being a particularly silly sort of trick, even then; but Murray assured me that the scenic effect was a striking one, and well worth experiencing, and I made up my mind to have a look, too.

Wilks didn't seem in any hurry to vacate, and Murray, who was getting more and more impatient at his selfishness, pinched his legs to fetch him down. The only effect was to cause Wilks to land out viciously with his foot, and with so much force and precision that it would have spoilt Murray's beauty considerably had the kick taken effect. We shouted up; but, what with his position and the row the train was making, it was evident that Wilks could not hear us.

'Oh, the pig!' grumbled Murray. 'Stick your head out of the window and tell him we want to have a go.'

I did so, and above the din of the train I caught the gist

of a wild tirade which brought me in again in double-quick time.

'What does he say?' queried Murray.

'Well, the printable part of it seems to be to the effect that he is wedged up somehow, and that you are a particular sort of ass for doing, or not doing, something or other that you should or shouldn't do,' said I. 'It is a bit disjointed and vague.'

'A big bit,' said Murray drily. 'Here, let's see what's up.'

Murray scrambled on to the seat and gave a mighty tug at Wilks' arm, at the same time yelling a frank and pointed suggestion to him to come in and let us have a go.

Then came down the answer, clear and unmistakable this time, and suggesting a world of latent wrath and some amount of pain.

'You fat-headed imbecile! don't mess about!' ran some of the tirade. 'Do you think I'm stopping here for the fun of it? I'm wedged up, I tell you, and can't get my head back anyway.'

Murray whistled.

'That's a jolly go,' he murmured rapturously. 'What are we going to do now? If his feet slip he'll be hanged, as sure as fate.'

He prodded Troddles in the ribs and told him to wake up for the execution, and Troddles did wake up. He grumbled a bit until he caught sight of the rigid and idiotic figure standing in the centre of the carriage, with his head through the hole in the top.

'What's Wilks doing there?' he inquired innocently.

'Admiring the scenery,' said Murray. 'He's been admiring it for the last ten minutes, and he'll have to go on doing it for the rest of his life. He's wedged, Troddles, dear. Got caught in, you know, and can't get out. Darned inconvenient thing, too, to have to drag a railway carriage round with you wherever you go for the rest of your days. Uncomfortable to sleep in, I should imagine. I wonder what they'll do? They might cut a piece out of the roof and let him have it for a collar on paying for the damage, I should think. The ring is set in an iron plate, if I know anything about it, and he'll just have to go on wearing it. Fancy, old Wilks might come to live in history, after all – the ass in the iron collar, a companion to the man in the iron mask.'

Murray's pleasantry struck us as being untimely, and we told him to shut up. It seemed to us much more important to give Wilks what assistance we could to help him out of his unpleasant predicament than to waste useful time in gibing at his misfortune; though I had some pretty severe things to say of the childish folly which had caused it. It was funny, I must admit, to see Wilks kick round when Murray tickled his legs, and endeavour to do some of us an injury; but that was also out of place, and I earnestly begged Murray to put the temptation on one side and give serious consideration to the problem of extracting him from the lamp-hole.

Murray was full of resource. When people get a tight ring on their finger, he told us, the usual way is to bind it round firmly with worsted or cotton, and then slip the end under the ring and wind it off. He said he didn't see why we couldn't adopt the same plan; we could wind Wilks up in the fishing-lines; but I didn't consider the plan practical, for obvious reasons. In fact, I thought it an unusually silly suggestion, even for Murray, and I said so, with the result that several useful minutes were lost in pointless recrimination.

Troddles said Wilks ought to move round a bit on his own account, and he pointed out, with some show of reason, that as there had been room for his head to go through there must obviously be room for it to come back again. He got up on the seat and hurled this truism through the roof to Wilks, who growled something inarticulate in reply, and kicked round a bit more just to show us that he was getting impatient and wanted a change of scene and position.

We got up to investigate, too, and by observation and inquiry we elicited the fact that Wilks was held a prisoner by his ears chiefly. He could get back as far as there, and then he wedged, and to try to force the passage was too painful for him to insist on after the first endeavour.

'That's the worst of having such lumping great flappers,' grumbled Murray. 'I always said he had too much ear, and if ever he got into a serious difficulty it would be either through them or his feet.'

Troddles suggested that one of us might climb up on to the roof and hold the projecting members flat while Wilks wriggled down. It was a practical scheme, but Troddles didn't rush to put it into operation, and we didn't feel quite equal to such a risky job as that, even in the sacred cause of friendship.

Murray said if it would rain or something, it would help, because cold made the flesh contract. I said so did a pair of scissors, and I put it to Wilks whether he had not better sacrifice a little superfluous ear and obtain liberty rather than remain fastened to a railway carriage for the rest of his life. As Murray said, there was such a lot of it that he could very well spare a square foot or so.

Wilks declined the proposal forcibly and none too politely, and just then we ran into Waltham Station. We crowded up round the door to discourage any possible passenger from entering; but a schoolboy, evidently going home after morning term, came to a halt in front of us, and, perhaps liking our appearance, resolved to travel in our company.

He was about fourteen, dressed in an untidy Eton suit, and with an engagingly dirty face, and he stood on the footboard and asked Murray plaintively if we wanted 'all the bally carriage' to ourselves. Murray was so staggered that he gave way and permitted the self-assured youngster to pass us, and he threw his belongings on to the rack and settled down, and produced his cigarette case and asked me to 'have a weed.'

Then the train moved out, and at the same time our small friend caught sight of the lower portion of Wilks and got interested.

'What's he doing?' he queried.

'Mending the roof,' said Murray, mendaciously.

'Rats!' quoth the cheeky youngster. 'He's been sticking his head out, and got it jammed. They all do that, unless they're in the know. We get all the new boys to do it, and then tickle 'em until they buy off. It's no end of a lark; let's try it on him.'

This facetious suggestion was accompanied by a significant upward gesture towards Wilks so that there should be no mistake as to who was meant.

We declined to experiment. It wasn't safe, we told him, and seeing that no fun was likely to be forthcoming, our small friend good-naturedly condescended to entertain us with anecdotes and illustrations of his school life and companions instead, though I could see that we had dropped considerably in his estimation.

50

This was slow for Wilks, and, after a few minutes, a chance though well-directed kick, which reached Troddles' ribs and made him sing out, apprised us that something was required from above.

'Well, I'm sugared!' said Murray, after listening intently. 'He says he wants a smoke.'

'He'll have to go on wanting,' I observed. 'How does he suppose he's going to get his pipe up there?'

'Hook it on to your fishing rod, ready lit, and drop it over to him from the window, why don't you?' advised our companion.

What that boy didn't know was clearly not worth knowing, and young as he was, he gave magnificent promise of being the sort of companion who would be likely to prove useful in a tight place.

Troddles hooked Wilks' pipe and pouch out of his pocket, and getting it under full steam he handed it to Murray, who fastened it to my rod, and ran a frightful risk of decapitation before he finally came to the conclusion that the plan wasn't feasible. Wilks couldn't do a blessed thing to help himself; and being compelled to cast in the dark, so to speak, it required a skill beyond what we possessed to drop the pipe anywhere near Wilks' mouth though we got it in his eye very successfully, once.

'Oh, well,' said the kid, not to be beaten, 'tell him to shift his long neck, and pass it up the side to him.'

Murray tried again, and after burning Wilks under the chin we contrived to effect the manoeuvre, and Wilks got his smoke.

It must have looked comical, and Troddles was saddened to think that he had left his outfit at home, and so lost the chance of obtaining a snap-shot of it.

The railway people were quite unnecessarily cross about the matter. Of course, it was silly of Wilks, but he knew that well enough without telling him so, and no one could have supposed that he did it just to vex other people. I know that it gave the porters a lot of trouble. They hung on to his legs and bawled at him savagely at first, until Wilks kicked the guard in the jaw and told them that he wasn't going to have his head tugged off just to save them a bit of trouble. They had to break up the train to get the carriage out and run it on to a siding, and then settle down to the business seriously. But it was of no use. Wilks was sore in neck and temper, he wouldn't even try half the likely schemes they propounded, and at last the station-master went off for a carpenter.

'Why not leave him as he is, and show him at a penny a time?' suggested our schoolboy companion, who had alighted with us and stayed by to see the thing out.

We said we wanted him for other purposes, or else we would.

'Oh,' said the boy coolly. 'Well, why don't you get him out, then?'

This was irritating; but Troddles who is generally kind to children, thoughtfully went over the whole thing again and tried to make the kid realise that we didn't because we couldn't.

'Rats!' retorted the animated lump of impudence. 'Tell him to hold his head on one side and draw it down until one ear is disengaged, and then cant over, and he'll come out like greased lightning. You don't need to go cutting up a good railway carriage for a simple thing like that.'

Wisdom from the mouth of babes!

The thing was so obviously simple that I wondered how on earth we could have failed to see it. All the same, I felt a painful desire to get that boy by the ear and pull it just to freshen up his sense of what is due to his elders, and to warn him not to be selfish in future in withholding the tidings of a great device or invention in times of emergency.

Late as it was, having got it, we weren't too uppish to take it. No more was Wilks, and a few minutes more sufficed to put him – raw and bruised from his struggles – inside the carriage again. He seemed to bear us a grudge for the whole thing – as if it had been our fault. As Murray said, if he didn't care about travelling that way, what on earth did he do it for?

Just then the boy, who was looking out of the window, turned round, and remarked casually.

'Here's the station-master coming back with the workman. He's got a slop with him, too, and if I were you I should do a guy out of the door on the off-side, and send my regrets on a post card.'

We gathered up our goods in double sharp time, and scrambled on to the line, boy and all. We just stayed to fasten the door again, and then made tracks in single file across the coal siding over a low fence and out on to the public road.

And that is how we went fishing on that eventful Saturday afternoon, and the only thing caught was a stiff neck and a cold in the left eye – by Wilks.

ON DRY COW FISHING

by Rudyard Kipling

ON DRY COW FISHING

It must be clearly understood that I am not at all proud of this performance. In Florida men sometimes hook and land, on rod and tackle a little finer than a steam-crane and chain, a mackerel-like fish called 'tarpon,' which sometimes run up to 120 lb. Those men stuff their captures and exhibit them in glass cases and become puffed up. On the Columbia River sturgeon of 150 lb. weight are taken with the line. When the sturgeon is hooked the line is fixed to the nearest pine tree or steamboat wharf, and after some hours or days the sturgeon surrenders himself, if the pine or line do not give way. The owner of the line then states on oath that he has caught a sturgeon, and he, too, becomes proud.

These things are mentioned to show how light a creel will fill the soul of a man with vanity. I am not proud. It is nothing to me that I have hooked and played 700 lb. weight of quarry. All my desire is to place the little affair on record before the mists of memory breed the miasma of exaggeration.

The minnow cost eighteenpence. It was a beautiful quill minnow, and the tackle-maker said that it could be thrown as a fly. He guaranteed further in respect to the triangles – it glittered with triangles – that, if necessary, the minnow would hold a horse. A man who speaks too much truth is just as offensive as a man who speaks too little. None the less, owing to the defective condition of the present law of libel, the tackle maker's name must be withheld.

The minnow and I and a rod went down to a brook to attend to a small jack who lived between two clumps of flags in the most cramped swim that he could select. As a proof that my intentions were strictly honourable, I may mention that I was using a light split-cane rod – very dangerous if the line runs through weeds, but very satisfactory in clean water, inasmuch as it keeps a steady strain on the fish and prevents him from taking liberties. I had an old score against the jack. He owed me two live bait already, and I had reason to suspect him of coming upstream and interfering with a little bleak pool under a horsebridge which lay entirely beyond his sphere of legitimate influence. Observe, therefore, that my tackle and my motives pointed clearly to jack, and jack alone; though I knew that there were monstrous big perch in the brook.

The minnow was thrown as a fly several times, and, owing to my peculiar, and hitherto unpublished, methods of fly throwing, nearly six pennyworth of the triangles came off, either in my coat collar, or my thumb, or the back of my hand. Fly fishing is a very gory amusement.

The jack was not interested in the minnow, but towards twilight a boy opened a gate of the field and let in some twenty or thirty cows and half a dozen cart horses, and they were all very much interested. The horses galloped up and down the field and shook the banks, but the cows walked solidly and breathed heavily, as people breathe who appreciate the Fine Arts.

By this time I had given up all hope of catching my jack fairly, but I wanted the live bait and bleak account settled before I went away, even if I tore up the bottom of the brook. Just before I had quite made up my mind to borrow a tin of chloride of lime from the farmhouse – another triangle had fixed itself in my fingers – I made a cast which for pure skill, exact judgement of distance, and perfect coincidence of hand and eye and brain, would have taken every prize at a bait casting tournament. That was the first half of the cast. The second was postponed because the quill minnow would not return to its proper place, which was under the lobe of my left ear. It had done thus before, and I supposed it was in collision with a grass tuft, till I turned round and saw a large red and white bald-faced cow trying to rub what would be withers in a horse with her nose. She looked at me reproachfully, and her look said as plainly as words: 'The season is too far advanced for gadflies. What is this strange disease?'

I replied, 'Madam, I must apologise for an unwarrantable liberty on the part of my minnow, but if you will have the goodness to keep still until I can reel in, we will adjust this little difficulty.'

I reeled in very swiftly and cautiously, but she would not wait. She put her tail in the air and ran away. It was a purely involuntary motion on my part: I struck. Other anglers may contradict me, but I firmly believe that if a man had foul-hooked his best friend through the nose, and that friend ran, the man would strike by instinct. I struck, therefore, and the reel began to sing just as merrily as though I had caught my jack. But had it been a jack, the minnow would have come away. I told the tackle maker this much afterwards, and he laughed and made allusions to the guarantee about holding a horse.

Because it was a fat innocent she-cow that had done me no harm the minnow held – held like an anchor fluke in coral moorings – and I was forced to dance up and down an interminable field very largely used by cattle. It was like salmon fishing in a nightmare. I took gigantic strides, and every stride found me up to my knees in marsh. But the cow seemed to stake along the squashy green by the brook, to skim over the miry backwaters, and to float like a mist through the patches of rush that squirted black filth over my face. Sometimes we whirled through a mob of her friends – there were no friends to help me – and they looked scandalised; and sometimes a young and frivolous cart horse would join in the chase for a few miles, and kick solid pieces of mud into my eyes; and through all the mud, the milky smell of kine, the rush and the smother, I was aware of my own voice crying: 'Pussy, pussy, pussy! Pretty pussy! Come along then, puss-cat!' You see it is so hard to speak to a cow properly, and she would not listen – no, she would not listen.

Then she stopped, and the moon got up behind the bollards to tell the cows to lie down; but they were all on their feet, and they came trooping to see. And she said, 'I haven't had my supper, and I want to go to bed, and please don't worry me.' And I said, 'The matter has passed beyond any apology. There are three courses open to you, my dear lady. If you'll have the common sense to walk up to my creel I'll get my knife and you shall have all the minnow. Or, again, if you'll let me move across to your near side, instead of keeping me so coldly on your off side, the thing will come away in one tweak. I can't pull it out over your withers. Better still, go to a post and rub it out, dear. It won't hurt much, but if you think I'm going to lose my rod to please you, you are mistaken.' And she said, 'I don't understand what you are saying. I am very, very unhappy.' And I said: 'It's all your fault for trying to fish. Do go to the nearest gate-post, you nice fat thing, and rub it out.'

For a moment I fancied she was taking my advice. She ran away, and I followed. But all the other cows came with us in a bunch, and I thought of Phaeton trying to drive the Chariot of the Sun, and Texan cowboys killed by stampeding cattle, and 'Green Grow the Rushes, oh!' and Solomon and Job, and 'loosing the bands of Orion,' and hooking Behemoth, and Wordsworth who talks about whirling round with stones and rocks and trees, and 'Here we go round the Mulberry Bush,' and 'Pippin Hill,' and 'Hey Diddle Diddle,' and most especially the top joint of my rod. Again she stopped – but nowhere in the neighbourhood of my knife – and her sisters stood moonfaced round her. It seemed that she might, now, run towards me, and I looked for a tree, because cows are very different from salmon, who only jump against the line, and never molest the fisherman. What followed was worse than any direct attack. She began to buck-jump, to stand on her head and her tail alternately, to leap into the sky, all four feet together, and to dance on her hind legs. It was so violent and improper, so desperately unladylike, that I was inclined to blush, as one would blush at the sight of a prominent statesman sliding down a fire escape, or a duchess chasing her cook with a skillet. That flopsome *abandon* might go on all night in the lonely meadow among the mists, and if it went on all night – this was pure inspiration – I might be able to worry through the fishing line with my teeth.

Those who desire an entirely new sensation should chew with all their teeth, and against time, through a best waterproofed silk line, one end of which belongs to a mad cow dancing fairy rings in the moonlight; at the same time keeping one eye on the cow and the other on the top joint of a split cane rod. She buck-jumped and I bit on the slack just in front of the reel; and I am in a position to state that

that line was cored with steel wire throughout the particular section which I attacked. This has been formally denied by the tackle maker, who is not to be believed.

The *wheep* of the broken line running through the rings told me that henceforth the cow and I might be strangers. I had already bidden good-bye to some tooth or teeth; but no price is too great for freedom of the soul.

'Madam,' I said, 'the minnow and 20 ft. of very superior line are your alimony without reservation. For the wrong I have unwittingly done to you I express my sincere regret. At the same time, may I hope that Nature, the kindest of nurses, will in due season. . . .'

She or one of her companions must have stepped on her spare end of the line in the dark, for she bellowed wildly and ran away, followed by all the cows. I hoped the minnow was disengaged at last; and before I went away looked at my watch, fearing to find it nearly midnight. My last cast for the jack was made at 6.23 p.m. There lacked still three-and-a-half minutes of the half hour; and I would have sworn that the moon was paling before the dawn!

'Simminly someone were chasing they cows down to bottom o' Ten Acre,' said the farmer that evening. 'Twasn't you sir?'

'Now under what earthly circumstances do you suppose I should chase your cows? I wasn't fishing for them, was I?'

Then all the farmer's family gave themselves up to jam-smeared laughter for the rest of the evening, because that was a rare and precious jest, and it was repeated for months, and the fame of it spread from that farm to another, and yet another at least 3 miles away, and it will be used again for the benefit of visitors when the freshets come in the spring.

But to the greater establishment of my honour and glory I submit in print this bald statement of fact, that I may not, through forgetfulness, be tempted later to tell how I hooked a bull on a Marlow Buzz, how he ran up a tree and took to water, and how I played him along the London road for 30 miles, and gaffed him at Smithfield. Errors of this kind may creep in with the lapse of years, and it is my ambition ever to be a worthy member of that fraternity who pride themselves on never deviating by one hair's breadth from the absolute and literal truth.

THE LEGACY OF NOAH'S ART

by Harry Graham

THE LEGACY OF NOAH'S ART

I

Besides being the most ancient and honourable of all human pastimes, fishing is the only form of sport that has been continuously practised without a break since the very creation of the universe.

The climatic conditions that prevailed at the time of the Flood rendered it almost impossible for the sportsmen of that period to take part in those pursuits to which Adam and his immediate descendants had devoted so much of their leisure in those happy days when the Eden coverts were still carefully preserved. The persistent succession of rainy days made deerstalking an unpleasant as well as an unprofitable amusement; as the tide gradually rose it became too damp for anything but snipe-shooting and otter-hunting, and, finally, when nearly the whole surface of the world had been submerged, every variety of game was driven to the mountain tops, where they clustered together in pathetic groups which could prove tempting to none but the most flagrant pot-hunter. It is said that when the flood eventually reached the summit of Mount Ararat, that eminence was so thickly infested with big game that it would have been impossible to throw one's hat out of any window of the ark without hitting a wild animal of some kind or another, and a shot fired at random 'into the brown' would have brought down at least a dozen specimens of the world's rarest *fauna*.

The prospect of anything in the form of a massacre was not likely to appeal to so thorough a sportsman as Noah, and when that worthy man had stowed his menagerie safely on board the ark he turned his whole attention to the capture of those denizens of the briny deep upon which his party was fated to rely for sole subsistence until the waters had sensibly subsided. It is, indeed, largely due to the fish diet upon which Noah and his family lived at this period that their descendants have acquired that colossal brain power which finds its expression today within the covers of such a volume as the reader now holds in his hand.

The modern angler, who delicately throws a 'dry fly' over some translucent, willow-fringed trout stream, may sneer at the ponderous piscatorial methods of his less dexterous ancestors. But it must always be remembered that at the time when Noah fished for his daily bread – or, rather, his daily bream – there was not a single dry fly to be had. The only two flies resident in the Ark had got thoroughly wet through long before they came on board, and to supply the existing deficiency of bait by sacrificing one of these valuable lepidoptera, upon whose survival the whole future of their race depended, would in any case have been the height of folly.

That some such solution of the problem crossed the mind of Japhet (the expert fisherman of the party) we have good reason for believing. As he turned a contemplative eye upon the various animals in his charge, seeking to determine which of them would prove the most suitable decoration for the bare fish-hook that he held in his hand, a perceptible shudder ruffled the surface of that sheltered community; the two worms who were lying half asleep in an upper bunk on the saloon deck, huddled more closely together for mutual comfort and support; the breathing of the ants came quick and sharp; and you could almost hear the beating of the caterpillars' hearts. It was, indeed, an auspicious moment for all the inmates of that floating palace, where so many couples lived together in what Ham facetiously described as '*canoe*bial bliss,' when the female wasp of the establishment unexpectedly became the happy mother of thirty fine boy grubs, several of whom it was rightly deemed permissible to make use of as ground-bait.

From that moment the Ark was always well provided with fresh food; its human inhabitants spent many happy hours fishing over the side, and, like that eminent British angler whose name is now a household word (though for the moment I cannot recollect it), found this edifying pastime 'a rest to the mind, a cheerer of the spirits, a diverter of sadness, a moderator of passions, a producer of contentedness, and a begetter of those habits of peace and perseverance upon which so much of human felicity depends.'

Thus it was that fishing became a universally popular pursuit; Japhet's creel fell upon the shoulders of a long line of worthy successors, from St. Peter to Sir Henry Wotton, from Mr. Isaak Walton to Sir Edward Grey and Mr. Harry Tate, and thence to my uncle, Sir Noel Biffin, than who (or "whom," if you prefer to be ungrammatical) no modern angler ever watched a float or impaled a worm upon a bent pin with greater patience or precision.

II

The subject of fishing divides itself naturally under four headings: tackle, bait, modes of procedure, and – I shall remember the fourth presently. Of these the first, though undoubtedly the most important, is by no means the easiest upon which to dogmatise satisfactorily.

It must, of course, be obvious that no two kinds of fish, and no two methods of angling demand the use of the same tackle; that it would be as foolish to trawl for tarpon with a light ten-foot split-cane trout rod and a thin horsehair cast, as it would be to sniggle for lithe and saith (whatever these may be) with a wire cable attached to a hop-pole. To dwell upon a commonplace of this kind would be to waste my valuable time and weary the reader, and though the latter be a minor consideration, it is one which in certain circumstances should not be entirely overlooked. It will therefore be sufficient for my purpose to limit this dissertation upon fishing tackle to a few words of counsel and warning, based upon a wide experience of every form and variety of angling gear with which it has been my good fortune to become acquainted in the course of a long and (I trust) not altogether futile career.

Whether ordinary horsehair or the gut of the silkworm provides the best material for those 'casts' or 'traces' (as they are sometimes called), upon which the angler must to so great an extent rely for any success that he may achieve with rod and line, is a mere matter of individual taste. Some experts hold one view, while others (equally worthy, honourable, and scrupulous men) feel bound to maintain a totally opposite opinion. I am personally inclined to support both parties; for although the product of the silkworm may be as hyaline and glabrous as any equine capillament, the latter may possess those sequaceous properties which counterbalance the natural lubricity that characterizes the former, and *vice versa*. But whichever form of material it is decided to make use of, the absolute necessity of exercising the greatest care and caution in its selection cannot be too strongly urged. If horsehair be chosen, it should be obtained from the tails of those massive steeds which are commonly harnessed to brewers' drays, and not on any account from cavalry chargers, pit ponies, or the emaciated crocks that still languish obscurely between the shafts of our obsolete hansom-cabs.

An excellent brand of horsehair is that which is supplied for surgical purposes, to stitch up wounds and so forth. In my youth I often obtained a stock of this material from a well-known chemist named Potasch, who kept a small shop in a by-street not far from Piccadilly Circus. The worthy druggist was himself a keen devotee of angling, and while waiting for my change I would constantly engage him in conversation upon the subject. It did not take me long to discover that he possessed all those moral qualities which are as useful to the fisherman as to the chemist: he was a philosopher, took a cheerful view of life, and had that happy knack of procuring the maximum amount of profit with the minimum of expenditure which is as much the key to success on the river bank as behind the counter of a druggery.

I remember being particularly struck on one occasion by his business methods. A rather seedy-looking individual entered the shop while I was there, and asked to be supplied with something that would cure indigestion. The chemist at once proceeded to concoct a pink mixture from the numerous large bottles that stood in a row on a long shelf behind him. To a little of the contents of a vessel labelled 'Grobelia Inflata' he added a few crystals of 'Hyp. Phos. Sod.,' poured in two or three drops of 'Aq. Pur.' and a dash of Tinct. Amm.,' measured out a dozen grains of 'Potass. Chlor.' and 'Tart. Ac.,' emptied the decoction into a small glass bottle, secured the cork with sealing wax and string, made a neat paper parcel of the whole thing, using more string and sealing wax, and handed it with a polite bow to his customer.

'How much?' the latter inquired gruffly.

'Two shillings, if you please,' said the druggist.

'Two shillings!' repeated the other indignantly. 'What on

earth do you take me for?'

With these words the man flung a threepenny bit upon the counter, picked up the bottle of medicine, and bolted from the shop.

I was naturally somewhat surprised by such extraordinary behaviour, but the chemist remained perfectly calm and unmoved. Shrugging his shoulders in a nonchalant manner, he turned to me with that charming smile which had won my heart the very first time I ever bought one of his porous plasters.

'After all,' he remarked philosophically, 'I've made twopence over the transaction, so I needn't complain.'

It is, as I have said, qualities such as my friend then displayed that make for success both in angling and drugging, and I was not surprised a year or two ago to learn that Mr Potasch was retiring from business an extremely wealthy man, and had been unanimously elected a Patron of the Home for Inebriate Fishermen which the late Sir Findon Haddough founded on the banks of the Thames. His name appeared in a prominent position among the knights in the last New Year's Honours List, and shortly afterwards, when I happened to attend the annual *conversazione* held at the Brighton Aquarium by the Association of Anglo-Saxon Anglers, I was delighted to notice, in a corner of the room, under the banner bearing the motto of the Association (*Non angeli sed angleri*), my old friends Sir Permanganate and Lady Potasch conversing affably with such eminent persons as Dr Nux and Lady Vomica Squills, and the Bishop of Soda and Mint.

The best way of procuring ordinary horsehair is for the angler, accompanied by a trusty friend, with their hats drawn well over their eyes, to hang about the threshold of some big brewery shortly after dawn. As the first waggon-load of casks issues from the gates, the fisherman should step nimbly forward and make a remark of a grossly offensive character to the leading drayman, dwelling perhaps on the latter's extraordinary resemblance to an organ-grinder's monkey, on his dubious parentage and obviously intemperate habits. Being a naturally passionate man, the driver will probably leap down from his perch without further ado, and offer to knock his traducer's head off. While the poor fellow is thus pleasantly engaged, and his attention has been temporarily diverted from his duties, the angler's accomplice should creep up behind the leading horse, wrench a handful of hair from that reluctant creature's tail, and escape at top speed into the offing, with his booty tightly clasped to his bosom. Later on in the day, when the angler has eventually calmed the indignant drayman by explaining to him that he mistook him for his brother, the two accomplices can meet at some appointed spot, and share the spoils without further interruption.

If, on the other hand, it is decided to use gut as the most efficient fabric for casts, there is no better way of ensuring the provision of perfect material than by keeping a small private herd of silkworms, from which the necessary product can be obtained fresh every day to meet the fisherman's requirements. These docile and industrious little creatures are very tame and easy to manage, will soon learn to eat mulberry leaves out of their master's hand, and can be taught to perform a number of entertaining tricks calculated to while away the longest winter evenings. At his fishing-box in Hampshire, my uncle, Sir Noel Biffin, reared a large flock of silkworms, each of whom he knew by name and grew so fond of that his face would often be suffused with tears when the gamekeeper informed him that the supply of gut was running short, and it became necessary to eviscerate another of his charming pets.

III

It is the greatest mistake to assume that any sort of line and any kind of gut is good enough to catch a fish with. It is, however, certainly true that in times of stress a broken cast has occasionally been satisfactorily mended with a boot-lace; and I have even heard tell of an angler who had left his tackle box at home spending a not altogether unprofitable morning fishing for eels with a pair of braces to which he had fastened a safety pin baited with a ham sandwich. Indeed, my uncle, Horace Biffin, never tires of repeating the story of the ten-pound grilse which he played for over three hours on the end of a thin line of twisted silk that he obtained in so curious a fashion as to merit description.

One summer's evening, two or three years ago, Uncle Horace made up a cheery little play-party, consisting of his wife, his sister Jane and myself, to visit that popular modern comedy, 'Infrequent Mary,' which was then being played to crowded houses at one of the best known of our West End theatres.

We were unable to get four stalls all together, but managed to secure two in the front row and two others immediately behind them. Uncle Horace was naturally averse from sitting next to his wife, and as the society of his sister seemed equally distasteful to him, the two ladies were persuaded to occupy the front seats, while the male members of the party sat in the two others in rear.

At the beginning of the second act I happened to notice that a small thread of silk was sticking out of the top of Aunt Sophie's gown at the back. I pointed this out to her husband, and he quickly leant forward and began very gently to pull it out. The thread, however, proved to be very much longer than he expected, and by the time Uncle Horace had extracted several feet of it and there was still no sign of his having reached the end, we realised that he was engaged upon a more arduous and complicated business than had originally been supposed. He would have preferred to avoid any further trouble by putting the thread back, but this was now impossible, and so, with clenched teeth and a determined look on his face, he set himself to reel out yard after yard of silk from the nape of his unconsious spouse's V-shaped bodice. Beyond giving an occasional wriggle, as though someone were tickling her, Aunt Sophie remained unmoved by (and apparently ignorant of) what was happening; she was indeed far too deeply engrossed in the play to appreciate the fact that her husband was producing miles of material from her neck in a fashion which riveted the attention of the other occupants of the theatre and would have made the most expert conjuror green with envy.

For close upon three-quarters of an hour Uncle Horace continued his self-imposed task, growing more and more exhausted as he hauled up furlong after furlong of the thread; while I encouraged and stimulated him by humming a sailor's chanty in his ear whenever he seemed to be flagging. At last the silk came to a sudden end. My companion sank back into his stall with a sigh of relief and his arms full of thread, and when we afterwards wound the latter into a ball it was found to measure no less than 4,637 1/4 yards in length.

During the interval between the last two acts of the play, Aunt Sophie repeatedly complained of the sudden coldness of the theatre, but gave no other sign that she was aware of anything remarkable having occurred. Uncle Horace, however, confided to me next day that when his wife reached home that night and began to undress she suddenly turned deadly pale, and rang for her maid.

It is impossible for me to repeat the conversation that ensued between these two estimable females on the subject of those intimate undergarments which my Aunt distinctly remembered having donned earlier in the evening, but which had now entirely and miraculously disappeared. Suffice it to say that to this day my poor relative imagines that when she dressed for dinner that night she must have been suffering from an attack of momentary mental aphasia, or she could certainly never have gone to the play in nothing but an evening gown, a petticoat, and a pair of stockings. Uncle Horace, of course, could easily have enlightened her, but there are some things that even the boldest husband shrinks from telling his wife, and one of these is that he intends to go fishing with a line of twisted silk composed exclusively of her *dessous*.

IV

It is generally advisable, if not absolutely necessary, for every angler to possess some slight knowledge of the theory and use of knots before he goes confidently forth to the chase. It will perpetually happen to him that he is called upon to join two lengths of gut together, to repair a broken line, attach hooks to casts, and so on; and clumsy fingers often entail the escape of a big fish and the loss of an expensive fly or a valuable bait.

Without becoming involved in an extensive dissertation on the properties of knots and the science of knotting, I may perhaps assume the truth of the self-evident proposition that, *if any plane closed curve have double points only, in passing continuously along the curve from one of these to the same again, an even number of double points has been passed through, and therefore knots which can be deformed into their own perversion may justly and without exaggeration be termed amphicheiral or even paradromic* – or indeed anything you like. This fact being once established, we may pass on to the consideration of a knot invented by my Uncle Noel, which fulfils all these conditions, has been found invaluable on a score of occasions, and can therefore be strongly recommended to the reader's notice. Once it has been tied – and I admit that this is a somewhat intricate business – there is no danger of its ever coming undone. Indeed, when an elderly clergyman whom I met once in Hertfordshire asked me to lace his footwear for him one Sunday morning as he did not wish to soil his fingers, my acquaintance with this particular knot enabled me to fasten his boots so securely that he was compelled to sleep in them for nearly a week, and his curate had finally to cut them off his feet in order to stave off imminent mortification.

I can best explain the 'Improved Biffin Knot,' as it is technically termed, by a simple diagram:

METHOD OF TYING.

AFTER TYING.

The method of tying this knot is as follows: *Form an overhand granny knot, pass the end round the standing part and through the bight, take two turns round the park and make a half-hitch through the standing part, lay each end over its own standing part and through the bight, under the standing part beyond the bight, and down through the bight over its own standing part and through the bight. Form a clove hitch with the loose ends, pass them through the bight and through each other, lay one of the ends over the knot beyond the standing part and over the bight, haul the ends taut, and the thing is done.*

Before quitting the subject of fishing tackle it may be as well to offer a word or two of advice upon the use of those waterproof boots, or 'waders', which form so necessary a part of every fly fisher's equipment.

The juvenile practice of donning one's father's best evening shoes, covering these with two pairs of stout stockings, and stepping boldy out into midstream with no further protection against the cold, is calculated to induce bronchial catarrh, scurvy, housemaid's knee, and kindred ailments which leave an indelible mark upon the most robust constitution.

In the heyday of my giddy youth I would often spend sixty or seventy hours a week standing up to my waist in water, flogging the surface of some icy torrent, without giving a thought to the possible evil effects of such foolhardy conduct. Experience has, however, shown me the folly of such proceedings, and today I never venture into the shallowest brook until I have carefully rubbed my feet with cod-liver oil, and encased my legs in thick waterproof waders reaching up to my neck.

Even so it is not always possible to avoid accidents. Once, for instance, when I was paternostering for pike in Perthshire, I inadvertently stepped into a deep hole in the river bed. The water immediately rushed in over the top of my waders, carrying with it a shoal of small minnows (or sticklebacks) that chanced to be in the vicinity. These creatures in their frantic efforts to escape, coursed madly round and round inside my boots, and so tickled and excoriated my legs that I became almost demented, and was afterwards laid up in bed for nearly three weeks with acute inflammation of the hips.

In order to guard against the recurrence of so unpleasant an experience I fastened a stout leather strap round the top of my waders before venturing upon another fishing expedition. The result of this nearly proved fatal. When trying to land a six-pound grayling, on the bonny, bonny banks of Loch Lomond, last spring, I overbalanced myself, lost my footing on a slippery rock, and fell headlong into the water. It is true that the strap round my chest prevented an inrush of fish, but it also checked any escape of air from my waders. The latter consequently became so inflated that they acted as lifebuoys and caused the lower part of my body to float on the top of the loch while my head remained immersed beneath its surface. I should have died miserably of suffocation but for the timely intervention of a passing shepherd, who mistook me for a German dirigible balloon that had been recently observed in the neighbourhood, gaffed me through the waders with his crook, and thus released the pent-up air and enabled me to resume that erect position which distinguishes so many human beings from some of the beasts that perish.

V

We now come to the question of bait, under which category I may include live-bait, dead-bait, white-bait, and the ordinary artificial fly with which every fisherman is familiar.

The choice of suitable bait requires the exercise of common sense as well as some slight knowledge of the habits of different fish. Although it is on record that a perch has been caught with its own eye baited on a hook, it would be crass stupidity for an angler to attempt a repetition of this feat. One might as well imagine that because a captured pike has been known to contain a grandfather's clock, a pianola, seventeen yards of blue ribbon, and a small corkscrew, it is therefore advisable to bait one's hook with a set of false teeth or a harpsichord. It should, however, be borne in mind that certain fish will only look at certain baits. Tarpon, for instance, are very particular as to the food they eat, and can be caught with nothing but the head of a red mullet. Parrot-fish, on the other hand, prefer hemp-seed to any other form of diet, while dogfish express a preference for mutton bones, and it would be futile to attempt to catch the smallest catfish (or kitten-fish, to be academically correct) with anything but bread and milk.

The most common type of live-bait is undoubtedly the ordinary earth- or lob-worm. This is justly considered a succulent morsel by almost every species of fish, and is at once hardy and easily procurable. On warm summer nights lobworms will be found in large quantities on any lawn or at the edge of garden paths, lying half out of their holes fanning themselves with a blade of grass, or bending gracefully over to slake their thirst with deep draughts of dew from the close-cropped turf at their feet. It then becomes a simple enough matter to creep up behind them in india-rubber tennis shoes, seize them smartly round the waist with the finger and thumb of the right hand, and transfer them to a jam pot or other suitable receptacle.

I have never denied that the threading of a worm upon a steel hook entails a certain amount of suffering, and to the sensitive mind such a process is inevitably fraught with unpleasantness. Mr. H. Cholmondeley-Pennell, perhaps the greatest human authority on bait, has done excellent work in the *Badminton Library* by deploring that unnecessary multiplication of hooks – a feature of the well-known 'Stewart' tackle – which, as he justly remarks, is apt to 'disfigure the worm and detract from its natural appearance.' No truer word was ever spoken. It requires but a slight effort of the imagination to understand that the too lavish use of hooks is the cause of many a domestic tragedy in the worm world. One can easily picture the return to her fireside of some punctured mother worm, so disfigured by the treatment she has received at human hands that her husband turns away from her in disgust, to transfer his affections elsewhere, while her children fly shrieking from the lawn.

When required for immediate use, worms should be kept in a tin box lined with moss, in which a little brick dust has been carefully sprinkled. This undoubtedly helps them to retain that ruddy, sunburnt complexion which will commend them to the consideration of the most fastidious fish. They should never be carried in the angler's mouth, nor in his trousers pocket with his loose change. Nothing is more tiresome than to be unable to articulate coherently when you desire to give an order to the gillie, and the latter may have justifiable cause for disappointment if, at the end of a long day's sport, a worm is pressed into his open palm in place of the gold coin with which it was the fisherman's intention to reward his services.

In most reputable angling clubs the use of ant's eggs as bait is strictly forbidden, partly because this particular lure is so deadly as to render the capture of fish a ridiculously easy affair, and partly because the robbing of ant-roosts has always been rightly regarded as a distinctly unchivalrous proceeding.

The legality of baiting a line with goldfish has not yet been seriously questioned, but I understand that there exists a strong feeling amongst conjurors that this form of bait should be illegitimatised. Professors of magic depend so entirely for their living upon a continuance of the world's supply of goldfish that they not unjustly claim that any action tending to the extermination of these animals is eminently prejudicial to their interests. There is, however, some talk of the matter being thrashed out in the law courts, where an appeal has already been lodged for what is legally known as the restitution of conjuror's rights, and while the question is *sub judice* it is obviously impossible to discuss it.

It should always be the fisherman's chief aim and object to keep his live-bait as fresh and lively as possible. For this purpose many authorities recommend the administration of small doses of alcohol. This, however, should not be given with too generous a hand, or the inebriated bait tends to become lachrymose and depressed, and the angler's ends are defeated. It is generally advisable to provide oneself with an additional ration of alcohol in case of emergency, since it demands a superhuman display of self-sacrifice to split one's last whisky-and-soda with a goldfish or apply one's favourite brandy flask to the lips of a swooning minnow. I am, personally, very punctilious in this matter, and never stir from the door until I am assured that a quart bottle of brandy is lying at the bottom of my creel. I must, nevertheless, confess that hitherto the worms in my bait-can have seen little more than the outside of the flagon.

VI

Within the limits of a single chapter it is impossible to deal at any length with the different methods of angling in vogue among fishermen in various portions of the world. But whether it be a man's intention to sniggle for carp, to boggle for bream, to trawl for conger, to blither for cod, to snood for smelts, or merely to plummet for plaice, there are certain rules which he should invariably observe if he wishes to fill his basket.

The bass (and its relative the double-bass) can be hooked with almost any tackle on any kind of a rod, but the deep-sea bass (or *basso profundo*) must always be played *con brio* below the line. In snaring skate, gunnel, octopi, or indeed any kind of ocean fish, from the homely haddock to the much maligned shed (whose position as the parent of the whitebait should surely entitle it to respect) a rod is far more effectual than a hand-line. With the latter it may sometimes happen, when a huge marine monster seizes the bait and bolts for the bed of the ocean at breakneck speed, that the line rushes out so rapidly through the fisherman's grasp as to cause the severest cuticular abrasion. The friction created is sometimes so great as to set the angler's hands on fire or even to amputate a finger.

A friend of mine was once dibbling for gunnets off the Isle of Wight, when an immense conger eel made off with his tackle, and before he could let go of the line his fingers had been completely severed at the knuckles, and fell with a series of dismal splashes into the sea. Portions of the missing limbs were subsequently recovered from the stomachs of various fish caught in the vicinity by the local fishermen, and it was a long time before the inhabitants of the island, as they sat round their humble boards of an evening, ceased to push away their plates of kedgeree untasted, remarking with some bitterness that my poor friend seemed to have a finger in every pie.

I need not point out the obvious dangers incurred by the deep-sea angler who fastens his hand-line to a waistcoat button and then goes to sleep at the bottom of the boat, relying upon being awakened by the struggle of some fish that has swallowed his bait. Should such a man accidentally hook a shark he stands a good chance of being pulled overboard, or, at any rate, of sharing a fate similar to that which befell the late Lord Bloxham, whose lamentable demise recently created so profound an impression upon London society.

'Beau' Bloxham will be remembered as one of the last survivals of those spacious days when members of the peerage were still regarded with respect by an admiring populace. He was always exquisitely groomed (as the lady novelists say) and dressed in a picturesque, if somewhat old-world, fashion. To see him strolling down to the House of Lords at four o'clock of an afternoon, to record his vote against the last legislative measure that had been passed by the House of Commons, exuding seals at every fob, with his shiny hat cocked saucily over one ear, was in itself a liberal sartorial education. It was Lord Bloxham's invariable habit to carry his latchkey in his right-hand trouser-pocket, on a long gold chain, the end of which was securely fastened to one of the buttons to which his braces were attached, and to this custom he owed his untimely decease.

One afternoon last summer, at about half past four, when his parliamentary duties had been punctiliously performed, Lord Bloxham returned home and proceeded in his usual leisurely fashion to insert his latchkey into the front door of Bloxham House, Grosvenor Square. By some unfortunate coincidence, for which Providence can alone be held responsible, Mrs Grindelbaum, who had been paying an afternoon call upon Lady Bloxham, happened at this moment to descend her ladyship's front staircase on her way out. The family butler, with that ceremonious air of a *grand seigneur* which he reserved for the titled and wealthy, flung the front door open for Mrs Grindelbaum to emerge, and the unwitting Lord Bloxham, chained to his latchkey, was precipitated into the front hall at an incredible rate of speed. Fortunately, the gold chain snapped, and like an arrow from the bow the aged peer flew from one end of the front hall to the other, cannoned off Mrs Grindelbaum on to the first footman, rebounded from the first footman on to the third footman, ricocheted off the third footman on to a priceless grandfather's clock, and, after finishing the last ten yards of the course on his back, was brought up short by a portrait of the first Earl of Bloxham (painted by Vandyke) which hung at the end of the passage.

Lord Bloxham was then in his eighty-first year and, being a man of economical habits, had made it his practice, ever since the imposition of the super-tax, to save wear and tear to his false teeth by carrying them in his coat-tail pocket between meals. In the course of their owner's flight across the front hall these articles came into violent contact with numerous pieces of furniture, and by the time Lord Bloxham reached the Vandyke he had been severely bitten no less than six times in various parts of his person. Medical aid was soon forthcoming, but in spite of the efforts of three well-known specialists in hydrophobia, and a visit to the Pasteur Institute in Paris, the patient's injuries proved fatal and he passed away, on his eighty-first birthday, universally mourned and regretted.

VII

In all forms of freshwater fishing concealment is the first requisite of sport. Salmon and trout are especially shy, and if they catch sight of an individual slinking along the river bank with a rod over his shoulder, the wiliest attempts to capture them will prove abortive. It is a very good plan in such circumstances to disguise oneself in the skin of a defunct cow (or horse), and trot along the margin of the stream, waving one's tail in the air and mooing (or neighing, as the case may be). But the difficulty of handling a trout rod effectively while running on all fours may easily be imagined, and on the whole perhaps the practice of getting oneself up to look like a willow, and weeping on the river bank, is to be preferred to the most lifelike bovine imitation.

It is not my intention to dwell upon those modern methods of scientific fishing which are so unsportsmanlike as to provoke the condemnation of all right-minded men. But I should be lacking in my duty to the reader if I forbore to mention the patent recently taken out by a French inventor for angling by means of a telephone – a system which would not be tolerated in any sporting country, and only requires to be described to earn universal reprobation.

Certain fish, it is well known, emit faint sounds when alarmed or distressed: tench continue to croak long after capture, and the herring when engaged in mutual intercourse with his fellows makes a noise like a bereaved mouse. Upon this well-known fact the Frenchman bases his invention, and has contrived an apparatus consisting of a telephone receiver and a detonator, both of which are sunk in the water and connected to a post of observation on the river bank. When any fish pass the receiver a sound of squeaking is distinctly heard above the buzzing of the local bees and the soughing of the trees. The angler thereupon presses a button, the detonator explodes, and the air is filled with fragments of dismembered fish, which can be collected at leisure in a landing net.

I only mention this form of angling to deplore it, being well aware that a slaughter such as I have described would evoke expressions of disgust from the least scrupulous of my readers.[*]

VIII

The true angler is usually a naturalist as well. He knows the name of every fly that he uses, and every fish that he catches, and will rightly hesitate to express his opinion of the latter's value in mere terms of the kitchen. Unlike the ignorant tiro, he will never throw away with every symptom of disgust a fine cuttlefish that has become entangled in his line. Being well acquainted with the various cephalopodous creatures from which the best marking-ink is manufactured, he takes them all carefully home and gets his wife to mark a dozen of his new evening shirts with them. Nothing escapes his vigilant eye: he studies the domestic life of every finny creature that moves beneath the face of the waters. He can discourse at length and with passionate eloquence upon the maternal habits of the cod, an animal that has no less than 3,687,760 children every year, and in this respect provides many of us with an example which, as Mr. Roosevelt has already declared, we should do well to follow if the human race is not to become extinct at no very distant date. His joys are simple joys, his pleasures simple pleasures. The confirmed angler leads an idyllic existence, surrounded by beautiful scenery, inhaling copious draughts of fresh air, and acquiring physical health at a very small financial outlay. He may employ his thoughts for hours at a time in the noblest studies, enjoy a close communion with nature, and cultivate those higher qualities of the mind that distinguish the fisherman from his less fortunate fellows. If he is unsuccessful from a sporting point of view he can always find comfort in the reflection that he has none to quarrel with but himself. If, on the other hand, he happens one day to stagger home with his basket bursting with fish, he will gain the universal esteem of his fellows, and as a respected member of some local *Angliars' Club* can devote the evening of his life to a meticulous narration of those tales of prowess with rod and line which even the most constant repetition can scarcely rob of their original audacity and imaginative splendour.

* The apparatus described above can be obtained for fifty-six francs (carriage paid) from M. Henri Blume, Rue de la Framboise, Aix-la-Chapelle, and I shall be obliged if readers will mention my name when ordering it. I speak from experience when I say that it will be found a most effective substitute for the mayfly, and provide the least competent sportsman with an original and inexpensive means of adding to his bag.

THE POACHER

Neil Munro

THE POACHER

The *Vital Spark* was lying at Greenock with a cargo of scrap iron, on the top of which was stowed loosely an extraordinary variety of domestic furniture, from bird cages to cottage pianos. Para Handy had just had the hatches off when I came to the quayside, and he was contemplating the contents of his hold with no very pleasant aspect.

'Rather a mixed cargo!' I ventured to say.

'Muxed's no' the word for't,' he said bitterly. 'It puts me in mind of an explosion. It's a flittin' from Dunoon. There would be no flittin's in the *Fital Spark* if she wass my boat. But I'm only the captain, och aye! I'm only the captain, thirty-five shullin's a week and liberty to put on a pea-jecket. To be puttin' scrap iron and flittin's in a fine smert boat like this iss carryin' coals aboot in a coach and twice. It would make any man use Abyssinian language.'

'Abyssinian language?' I repeated, wondering.

'Chust that, Abyssinian language – swearing and the like of that, you ken fine, yoursel', withoot me tellin' you. Fancy puttin' a flittin' in the *Fital Spark*! You would think she wass a coal-laary, and her with two new coats of pent out of my own pocket since the New Year.'

'Have you been fishing?' I asked, desirous to change the subject, which was, plainly, a sore one with the Captain. And I indicated a small fishing net which was lying in the bows.

'Chust the least wee bit touch,' he said, with a very profound wink. 'I have a bit of a net there no' the size of a pocket-naipkin, that I use noo and then at the river-mooths.

I chust put it doon – me and Dougie – and whiles a salmon or a sea-troot meets wi' an accident and gets into't. Chust a small bit of a net, no' worth speakin' aboot, no' mich bigger nor a pocket-naipkin. They'll be calling it a splash-net, you ken yoursel' withoot me tellin' you.' And he winked knowingly again.

'Ah, Captain!' I said, 'that's bad! Poaching with a splash-net! I didn't think you would have done it.'

'It's no' me; it's Dougie,' he retorted promptly. 'A fair duvvee for high jeenks, you canna keep him from it. I told him many a time that it wasna right, becaause we might be found oot and get the jyle for't, but he says they do it on aal the smertest yats. Yes, that iss what he said to me – "They do it on aal the first-cless yats; you'll be bragging the *Fital Spark* iss chust ass good ass any yat, and what for would you grudge a splash-net?" '

'Still it's theft, Captain,' I insisted. 'And it's very, very bad for the rivers.'

'Chust that!' he said complacently. 'You'll likely be wan of them fellows that goes to the hotels for the fushing in the rivers. There's more sport aboot a splash-net; if Dougie wass here he would tell you.'

'I don't see where the sport comes in,' I remarked, and he laughed contemptuously.

'Sport!' he exclaimed. 'The best going. There wass wan

time yonder we were up Loch Fyne on a Fast Day, and no' a shop open in the place to buy onything for the next mornin's breakfast. Dougie says to me, "what do you think yoursel' aboot takin' the punt and the small bit of net no' worth mentionin', and going doon to the river mooth when it's dark and seeing if we'll no' get a fush?"

' "It's a peety to be poaching on the Fast Day," I said to him.

' "But it's no' the Fast Day in oor parish," he said. "We'll chust give it a trial, and if there's no fush at the start we'll come away back again." Oh! a consuderate fellow, Dougie; he saw my poseetion at wance, and that I wasna awfu' keen to be fushin' wi' a splash-net on the Fast Day. The end and the short of it wass that when it wass dark we took the net and the punt and rowed doon to the river and began to splash. We had got a fine haul at wance of six great big salmon, and every salmon Dougie would be takin' oot of the net he would be feeling it all over in a droll way, till I said to him, "What are you feel-feelin' for, Dougie, the same ass if they had pockets on them? I'm sure they're all right."

' "Oh, yes," he says, "right enough, but I wass frightened they might be the laird's salmon, and I wass lookin' for the luggage label on them. There's none. It's all right; they're chust wild salmon that nobody planted."

'Weel, we had got chust ass many salmon ass we had any

need for whem somebody birled a whustle, and the river watchers put off in a small boat from a point outside of us to catch us. There wass no gettin' oot of the river mooth, so we left the boat and the net and the fush and ran ashore, and by-and-by we got up to the quay and on board the *Fital Spark*, and paaused and consudered things.

' "They'll ken it's oor boat," said Dougie, and his clothes wass up to the eyes in salmon scales.

' "There's no doo't aboot that," I says. "If it wassna the Fast Day I wouldna be so vexed; it'll be an awful disgrace to be found oot workin' a splash-net on the Fast Day. And it's peety aboot the boat, it wass a good boat, I wish we could get her back."

' "Ay, it's a peety we lost her," said Dougie; "I wonder in the wide world who could have stole her when we were doon the fo'c'sle at oor supper?" Oh, a smart fellow, Dougie! when he said that I saw at wance what he meant.

' "I'll go up this meenute and report it to the polis office," I said quite firm, and Dougie said he would go with me too, but that we would need to change oor clothes, for they were covered with fush-scales. We changed oor clothes and went up to the sercheant of polis, and reported that somebody had stolen oor boat. He wass sittin' readin' his Bible, it bein' the Fast Day, wi' specs on, and he kneeked up at us, and said, "You are very spruce, boys, with your good clothes on at this time of the night."

' "We aalways put on oor good clothes on the *Fital Spark* on a Fast Day," I says to him; "it's as little as we can do, though we don't belong to the parish."

'Next day there wass a great commotion in the place aboot some blackguards doon at the river mooth poachin' with a splash-net. The Factor wass busy, and the heid gamekeeper wass busy, and the polis wass busy. We could see them from the dake of the *Fital Spark* goin' aboot buzzin' like bumbees.

' "Stop you!" said Dougie to me aal of a sudden. "They'll be doon here in a chiffy, and findin' us with them scales on oor clothes – we'll have to put on the Sunday wans again."

' "But they'll smell something if they see us in oor Sunday clothes," I said. "It's no' the Fast Day the day."

' "Maybe no' here," said Dougie, "but what's to hinder it bein' the Fast Day in oor own parish?"

'We put on oor Sunday clothes again, and looked the Almanac to see if there wass any word in it of a Fast Day any place that day, but there wass nothing in the Almanac but tides, and the Battle of Waterloo, and the weather for next winter. That's the worst of Almanacs; there's nothing in them you want. We were fair bate for a Fast Day any place, when The Tar came up and asked me if he could get to the funeral of a cousin of his in the place at two o'clock.

' "A funeral!" said Dougie. "The very thing. The Captain and me'll go to the funeral too. That's the way we have on oor Sunday clothes." Oh, a smert, smert fellow, Dougie!

'We had chust made up oor mind it wass the funeral we were dressed for, and no' a Fast Day any place, when the polisman and the heid gamekeeper came doon very suspeecious, and said they had oor boat. "And what's more," said the gamekeeper, "there's a splash-net and five stone of salmon in it. It hass been used, your boat, for poaching."

' "Iss that a fact?" I says. "I hope you'll find the blackguards," and the gamekeeper gave a grunt, and said somebody would suffer for it, and went away busier than ever. But the polis sercheant stopped behind. "You're still in your Sunday clothes, boys," said he; "what iss the occasion today?"

' "We're going to the funeral," I said.

' "Chust that! I did not know you were untimate with the diseased," said the sercheant.

' "Neither we were," I said, "but we are going oot of respect for Colin." And we went to the funeral, and nobody suspected nothin', but we never got back the boat, for the gamekeeper wass chust needin' wan for a brother o' his own. Och ay! there's wonderful sport in a splash-net.'

THE EVERLASTING ANGLER

Stephen Leacock

THE EVERLASTING ANGLER

The fishing season will soon be with us. For lovers of fishing this remark is true all the year round. It has seemed to me that it might be of use to set down a few of the more familiar fish stories that are needed by anyone wanting to qualify as an angler. There is no copyright on these stories, since Methuselah first told them, and anybody who wishes may learn them at least and make free use of them.

I will begin with the simplest and best known. Everybody who goes fishing has heard it, and told it a thousand times. It is called:

I

THE STORY OF THE FISH THAT WAS LOST

The circumstances under which the story is best told are these. The fisherman returns after his day's outing with his two friends whom he has taken out for the day, to his summer cottage. They carry with them their rods, their landing net and the paraphernalia of their profession. The fisherman carries also on a string a dirty looking collection of little fish, called by courtesy the 'catch.' None of these little fish really measures more than about seven-and-a-half inches long and four inches round the chest. The fisherman's wife and his wife's sister and the young lady who is staying with them come running to meet the fishing party, giving cries of admiration as they get sight of the catch. In reality they would refuse to buy those fish from a butcher at a cent-and-a-half a pound. But they fall into ecstasies and they cry, 'Oh, aren't they beauties? Look at this big one!' The 'big one' is about eight inches long. It looked good when they caught it, but it has been shrinking ever since, and it looks now as if it had died of consumption. Then it is that the fisherman says, in a voice in which regret is mingled with animation:

'Yes, but say, you ought to have seen the one that we lost. We had hardly let down our lines—'

But it may be interjected here that all fishermen ought to realise that the moment of danger is just when you let down your line. That is the moment when the fish will put up all kinds of games on you, such as rushing at you in a compact mass so fast that you can't take them in, or selecting the largest of their number to snatch away one of your rods.

'We had hardly let down our lines,' says the fisherman, 'when Tom got a perfect monster. That fish would have weighed five pounds – wouldn't it, Tom?'

'Easily,' says Tom.

'Well, Tom started to haul him in and he yelled to Ted and me to get the landing net ready and we had him right up to the boat, right up to the very boat' – 'Right up to the boat,' repeated Tom and Edward sadly – 'when the damn line broke and biff! away he went. Say, he must have been two feet long, easily two feet!'

'Did you see him?' asks the young lady who is staying with them. This of course she has no right to ask. It's not a fair question. Among people who go fishing it is ruled out. You may ask if a fish pulled hard, and how much it weighed, but you must not ask whether anybody *saw* the fish.

'We could see where he was,' says Tom.

Then they go on up to the house carrying the 'string' or 'catch' and all three saying at intervals: – 'Say! if we had only landed that big fellow!'

By the time this anecdote has ripened for winter use, the fish will have been drawn actually into the boat (thus settling all question of seeing it), and will there have knocked Edward senseless, and then leaped over the gunwale.

II

STORY OF THE EXTRAORDINARY BAIT

This is a more advanced form of fishing story. It is told by fishermen for fishermen. It is the sort of thing they relate to one another when fishing out of a motor boat on a lake, when there has been a slight pause in their activity and when the fish for a little while – say for two hours – have stopped biting. So the fishermen talk and discuss the ways and means of their craft. Somebody says that grasshoppers make good bait; and somebody else asks whether any of them have ever tried Lake Erie softshell crabs as bait, and then one – whoever is lucky enough to get in first – tells the good old bait story.

'The queerest bait I ever saw used,' he says, shifting his pipe to the other side of his mouth, 'was one day when I was fishing up in one of the lakes back in Maine. We'd got to the spot and got all ready when we suddenly discovered that we'd forgotten the bait—'

At this point any one of the listeners is entitled by custom to put in the old joke about not forgetting the whisky.

'Well, there was no use going ashore. We couldn't have got any worms and it was too early for frogs, and it was ten miles to row back home. We tried chunks of meat from our lunch, but nothing doing! Well, then, just for fun I cut a white bone button off my pants and put it on the hook. Say!

you ought to have seen those fish go for it. We caught, oh, easily twenty – yes, thirty – in about half an hour. We only quit after we'd cut off all our buttons and our pants were falling off us! Say, hold on, boys, I believe I've got a nibble! Sit steady!'

Getting a nibble of course will set up an excitement in any fishing party that puts an end to all storytelling. After they have got straight again and the nibble has turned out to be 'the bottom' – as all nibbles are – the moment would be fitting for any one of them to tell the famous story called:

III

BEGINNER'S LUCK, OR THE WONDERFUL CATCH MADE BY THE NARRATOR'S WIFE'S LADY FRIEND

'Talking of that big catch that you made with the pants button,' says another of the anglers, who really means that he is going to talk of something else, 'reminds me of a queer thing I saw myself. We'd gone out fishing for pickerel, 'Dorés' they call them up there in the lake of Two Mountains. We had a couple of big row boats and we'd taken my wife and the ladies along – I think there were eight of us, or nine perhaps. Anyway, it doesn't matter. Well, there was a young lady there from Dayton, Ohio, and she'd never fished before. In fact she'd never been in a boat before. I don't believe she'd ever been near the water before.'

All experienced listeners know now what is coming. They realize the geographical position of Dayton, Ohio, far from the water and shut in everywhere by land. Any prudent fish would make and sneak for shelter if he knew that a young lady from Dayton, Ohio, was after him.

'Well, this girl got an idea that she'd like to fish and we'd rigged up a line for her just tied on to a cedar pole that we'd cut in the bush. Do you know, you'd hardly believe that girl had hardly got her line into the water when she got a monster. We yelled to her to play it or she'd lose it, but she just heaved it up into the air and right into the boat. She caught seventeen, or twenty-seven, I forget which, one after the other, while the rest of us got nothing. And the fun of it was she didn't know anything about fishing, she just threw the fish up into the air and into the boat. Next day we got her a decent rod with a reel and gave her a lesson or two and then she didn't catch any.'

I may say with truth that I have heard this particular story told not only about a girl from Dayton, Ohio, but about a girl from Kansas, a young lady just out from England, about a girl fresh from Paris, and about another girl, not fresh – the daughter of a minister. In fact, if I wished to make sure of a real catch, I would select a girl fresh from Paris or New York and cut off some of my buttons, or hers, and start to fish.

IV

THE STORY OF WHAT WAS FOUND IN THE FISH

The stories, however, do not end with the mere catching of the fish. There is another familiar line of anecdote that comes in when the fish are to be cleaned and cooked. The fishermen have landed on the rocky shore beside the rushing waterfall and are cleaning their fish to cook them for the midday meal. There is an obstinate superstition that fish cooked thus taste better than first-class kippered herring put up in a tin in Aberdeen where they know how. They don't, but it is an honourable fiction and reflects credit on humanity. What is more, all the fishing party compete eagerly for the job of cutting the insides out of the dead fish. In a restaurant they are content to leave that to anybody sunk low enough and unhappy enough to have to do it. But in the woods they fight for the job.

So it happens that presently one of the workers holds up some filthy specimen of something in his hand and says, 'Look at that! See what I took out of the trout! Unless I mistake it is part of a deer's ear. The deer must have stooped over the stream to drink and the trout bit his ear off.'

At which somebody – whoever gets it in first – says:

'It's amazing what you find in fish. I remember once trolling for trout, the big trout, up in Lake Simcoe and just off Eight-Mile Point we caught a regular whopper. We had no scales, but he weighed easily twenty pounds. We cut him open on the shore afterwards, and say – would you believe it? – that fish had inside him a brass buckle – the whole of it – and part of a tennis shoe, and a rain-check from a baseball game, and seventy-five cents in change. It seems hard to account for it, unless perhaps he'd been swimming round some summer hotel.'

These stories, I repeat, may now be properly narrated in the summer fishing season. But of course, as all fishermen know, the true time to tell them is round the winter fire, with a glass of something warm within easy reach, at a time when statements cannot be checked, when weights and measures must not be challenged and when fish grow to their full size and their true beauty. It is to such stories as these, whether told in summer or in winter, that the immemorial craft of the angler owes something of its continued charm.

A CORNER IN WORMS

William Cain

A CORNER IN WORMS

My old friend Wiernershnizel – I should say Wynne, for that is how he prefers nowadays to see his name spelt – is the proprietor of one of the oldest-established and most reputable bucket-shops in Copthall Avenue. There is no shrewder man of business in the City. Never once has Wynne been in jail. I can't tell you how often they have tried to put him there, but he has done them every time. I tell you, he is clever. But it is not with Wynne as a man of business that I am concerned.

He has another side. You will never guess what it is, so I may as well tell you. He is a sportsman to the core of his being. Yes, this astute, rapacious adventurer of the Stock Markets is a sea angler of the most earnest description. Not a Sunday passes from January to December without witnessing the arrival of my dear old Wynne, loaded with his rods, his paternoster, and his bait-cans, upon the point of Brighton, Deal, or some other pier. He is as indefatigable as he is regular; always the first angler to arrive, he is ever the last to depart. You would hardly know Wynne at these times. He is no longer the keen man of business, with an eye open singly to the main chance; he is the sportsman, with a soul aflame for the capture and destruction of dabs, gurnards, and starfish. Business affairs, though in their way splendid enough, are, after all, sordid when compared with the things (whatever they may be) which occupy the thoughts of the sea angler.

That the thoughts of Wynne are not sordid when he is fishing is pretty conclusively proved by the fact that he never catches anything at all except, now and then, the girders of a pier or somebody else's bait. Never yet has he landed a fish. He is either the most unlucky or most incompetent sea angler in Great Britain; that is clear. But what I say is, a man who can go on fishing year after year, winter and summer, rain or shine, storm or calm, freezing or boiling, with never a fin to show for it, cannot – I say he cannot – be actuated by motives of gain. Such a man can be nothing but a sportsman of the very purest ray. It is obvious.

I hope you won't think that I reflect upon his sportsmanship when I tell you that Wynne has nearly all his life cherished the ambition to obtain a prize in an angling tournament. That doesn't dim his lustre for you, I believe. It should, on the contrary, brighten it. If it were a mere suitcase or tantalus that he was after, it might dim him, I admit. But, to think that, would be to wrong Wynne grievously. He has all the suitcases and tantaluses he can possibly require. Prizes to a man like Wynne are symbols merely. They are glory in material form. It has been glory – reputation – that Wynne has been after all these years.

He wants to be pointed out in Lothbury as the man who, for example, came out top of thirty thousand at Bexhill, or the man who broke all the records for Pegwell Bay, or the man who landed the biggest known codling at Broadstairs in August. That's all he wants. Anyone else may have the barometers and the brandy flasks.

I repeat, the man is a sportsman, through and through.

Now listen to this and tell me if you think there is anything sordid or material about Wynne – Wynne the angler, I mean, of course.

A few months ago the championships of Goodwin's Bay were about to be held, and Wynne (who belongs to every sea angling club in Southeastern England) had entered his name as usual and for every event. Some weeks before the date that had been fixed he had what is at present called a brainstorm. He had just made a hundred and twenty thousand pounds, he and several associates having engineered a highly successful corner in calico. His thoughts were naturally attuned to the engineering of corners. And so while he was furbishing up his tackle one evening for the coming contest at Goodwin's Bay, he suddenly slapped his knee and cried: 'Eureka!' He didn't know what Eureka means; he only knew that it is the proper exclamation with which to hail the birth of a bright idea.

And what was his bright idea?

Nothing less than to go down to Goodwin's Bay, just before the meeting, and corner lug and rag.

What, pray, is lug? What may rag be?

Lug, my poor friend, is an obscene and hairy worm, about as long as your foot, which lurks in the sand and is dug up and dragged out in hundreds by the longshoremen and sold to sea anglers for bait. Rag is another outrage of the same kind. It differs from lug only in the degree of its obscenity.

Lug and rag are odious-looking creatures, but the fishes love them, and the sea anglers swear by them, beyond all other baits. In fact, without a large supply of lug and rag no sea angler will approach the ocean with any kind of confidence. To be without lug or rag is, to the sea angler, almost what to be without cartridges is to the gunner, or to be without beer is to the yachtsman.

Do you grasp the significance of Wynne's project now? I hope so. You see – don't you? – that if he could secure all the available supplies of lug and rag for the day of the championships he would be in an almost unassailable position. No one else would have a chance against him.

I maintain, therefore, that for a brainstorm Wynne's brainstorm was something like a brainstorm.

He did this thing. He turned over all the bucket-selling to his partner, went down to Goodwin's Bay three clear days before the date of the competition, and got into touch with the entire bait-digging population of the place. When, on the eve of the contest, he rested from his labours, he had contracts in his pocket covering the entire local harvest of lug and rag for the succeeding twenty-four hours. This, I may tell you, cost him a good deal in earnest money; but what were trouble and money to Wynne when his reputation as a sportsman was concerned? Nothing. Nothing whatever.

You are to know that lug and rag can only be delved out

of the sands when the tide is out. You are also to know that the competition was timed to last from 10.30 a.m. to 4.30 p.m., when there would be water under the whole length of the pier, and, consequently, over those sands where dwell the worms aforesaid. Of all this Wynne was well aware; indeed, his whole scheme depended on it. He was quite certain of his ground, because these tidal arrangements are not accidental. The officials of Trinity House decide them in consultation with the editor of Whitaker's Almanack and the secretary of the British Sea Anglers' Association. Oh! Wynne knew exactly what he was doing.

Day dawned upon the backs of a hundred and fifty longshoremen howking out the lug and rag from their holes. When the tide flowed and interrupted their labours the number of the worms which were held at Wynne's sole disposal staggers belief and imagination.

Wynne, furnished with a large bag of coin, stood at the foot of the pier; one by one the longshoremen brought him their treasure and poured it out of buckets into the bait-cans with which Wynne had surrounded himself. At last the final lug was delivered up, the ultimate rag exchanged for copper.

Wynne, owner of every sandworm in Goodwin's Bay, stood, master of the situation, to await the arrival of the sea anglers. Their train was due in at 10.12.

As for the longshoremen, having nothing more to do at the pier, these persons betook themselves to the drinking houses of Goodwin's Bay.

The 10.12 arrived, the sea anglers precipitated themselves out of the station and ran furiously to the pier, feeling in their pockets for money wherewith to purchase bait. They made no doubt, the unsuspecting wretches, that they would, as always upon this great day of the Goodwin's Bay year, be greeted with the lusty cry, from a hundred and fifty longshore throats, of, 'Fine lug, gentlemen, good rag, gentlemen! Six a penny! Good lug! Fine rag! Thirdeen fer tuppence!'

To their stupefaction there was not a single worm-merchant in sight. Only Wynne, the centre of bait-cans, stood by the turnstiles, hellishly smiling.

The sea anglers halted in a body, questioning with large eyes the meaning of this sinister spectacle. Then suddenly they realised what had happened (for sea anglers have brains, I may tell you), and at once they were again in motion, charging down upon Wynne with shouts of 'How much the lug? What price the rag?'

Wynne waved them away and held up his hand for silence. 'No price the lug,' he said. 'The rag is not for sale.'

A scream of anguish arose. Poor devils! they knew Wynne's City reputation, and they understood that they were up against it. They wasted no time in supplication, but began instantly to bid against one another for the bait.

'I'll give you sixpence a dozen!' they shouted. 'I'll give a shilling. Two shillings. Half a crown. Five bob.'

Now this is where the proof of Wynne's perfect sportsmanship appears. He had these men at his mercy. They were crazy for the lug and the rag, without which their angling must be a mockery. They were losing their heads all round him, offering shillings for penn'orths, bidding crowns for what had cost him but a copper or two. Yet he held to his purpose. He kept his vision. He stuck to his worms.

After that I imagine that you won't be inclined to think that there was very much sordidness about Wynne – I mean always Wynne the angler.

Presently the sea anglers understood that they were losing their time with Wynne. They began to scatter in search of longshoremen. The longshoremen were already beginning to straggle, refreshed, out of those places into which they had lately vanished. The sea anglers prostrated themselves before those longshoremen and begged for worms at any price. In vain.

Worms in Goodwin's Bay were 'off' until the tide should recede. And by that time the competition would have been fought out. Well, I don't want to linger over the sorrows of these poor men, and I don't want unduly to prolong this history. I was, after all, only concerned to show you how sportsmanship can ennoble a man, how it can purge him of all desire for material gain. I suppose Wynne could have made as much as two pounds ten, or perhaps even three pounds profit, if he had listened to the promptings of his mercantile instincts. He bade them be silent. He gave up gold for glory. Well, I say that was a fine thing, finely done. That's all. I only say that.

The pity is that Wynne should have got nothing out of it. He deserved better fortune. The fact remains that, for all his worms, he never caught a thing all day but a pair of old trousers. Awful old trousers they were, obviously discarded by a longshoreman, and a longshoreman, as is well known, has to be practically arrestable before he discards his trousers.

Yes, that's all that Wynne fished out of the sea, and with only a pair of trousers to show he could qualify for none of the prizes. Whereas (for no other sea angler, naturally, caught so much as a button) if he had managed to secure even a pale green crab he would have won every prize there was – for the greatest number of fishes, greatest aggregate weight, greatest average, heaviest single fish, and fish in best condition, as well as all the booby prizes for the smallest number, smallest aggregate weight, smallest average, lightest fish, shortest fish, and worst-conditioned fish. But it was not to be.

However, he has the consolation that he acted like a true sportsman. Of that Wynne is not to be robbed. And he is able, at any rate, to be pointed out in Threadneedle Street as the man who cornered worms.

That is, in a way, a distinction.

THE RIVER GOD

Roland Pertwee

THE RIVER GOD

When I was a little boy I had a friend who was a colonel.
He was not the kind of colonel you meet nowadays, who
manages a motor showroom in the West End of London

and wears crocodile shoes and a small moustache and who calls you 'old man' and slaps your back, independent of the fact that you may have been no more than a private in the war. My colonel was of the older order that takes a third of a century and a lot of Indian sun and Madras curry in the making.

A veteran of the Mutiny he was, and wore side whiskers to prove it.

Once he came upon a number of sepoys conspiring mischief in a byre with a barrel of gunpowder. So he put the butt of his cheroot into the barrel and presently they all went to hell. That was the kind of man he was in the way of business.

In the way of pleasure he was very different. In the way of pleasure he wore an old Norfolk coat that smelt of heather and brine, and which had no elbows to speak of. And he wore a Sherlock Holmesy kind of cap with a swarm of salmon flies upon it, that to my boyish fancy was more splendid than a crown. I cannot remember his legs, because they were nearly always under water, hidden in great canvas waders. But once he sent me a photograph of himself riding on a tricycle, so I expect he had some knickerbockers too, which would have been that tight kind, with box cloth under the knees.

Boys don't take much stock of clothes. His head occupied my imagination. A big, brave, white-haired head with cherry-red rugose cheeks and honest, laughing, puckered eyes, with gunpowder marks in their corners.

People at the little Welsh fishing inn where we met said he was a bore; but I knew him to be a god and shall prove it.

I was ten years old and his best friend.

He was seventy something and my hero.

Properly I should not have mentioned my hero so soon in this narrative. He belongs to a later epoch, but sometimes it is forgivable to start with a boast, and now that I have committed myself I lack the courage to call upon my colonel to fall back two paces to the rear, quick march, and wait until he is wanted.

The real beginning takes place, as I remember, somewhere in Hampshire on the Grayshott Road, among sandy banks, sentinel firs, and plum-coloured wastes of heather. Summer holiday time it was, and I was among folks whose names have since vanished like lizards under the stones of forgetfulness.

Perhaps it was a picnic walk; perhaps I carried a basket and was told not to swing it for fear of bursting its cargo of ginger beer. In those days ginger beer had big bulgy corks held down with string. In a hot sun or under stress of too much agitation the string would break and the corks fly. Then there would be a merry foaming fountain and someone would get reproached.

One of our company had a fishing rod. He was a young

man who, one day, was to be an uncle of mine. But that didn't concern me. What concerned me was the fishing rod, and presently – perhaps because he felt he must keep in with the family – he let me carry it.

To the fisherman born there is nothing so provoking of curiosity as a fishing rod in a case. Surreptitiously I opened the flap, which contained a small brass spear in a wee pocket, and, pulling down the case a little, I admired the beauties of the cork butt, with its gunmetal ferrule and reel rings and the exquisite frail slenderness of two top joints.

'It's got two top joints – two!' I exclaimed ecstatically.

'Of course,' said he. 'All good trout rods have two.'

I marvelled in silence at what seemed to me then a combination of extravagance and excellent precaution.

There must have been something inherently understanding and noble about that young man who would one day be my uncle, for, taking me by the arm, he sat me down on a tuft of heather and took the pieces of rod from the case and fitted them together.

The rest of the company moved on and left me in paradise.

It is thirty-five years ago since that moment and not one detail of it is forgotten. There sounds in my ears today as clearly as then the faint, clear pop made by the little cork stoppers with their boxwood tops as they were withdrawn. I remember how, before fitting the pieces together, he rubbed the ferrules against the side of his nose to prevent them sticking. I remember looking up the length of it through a tunnel of sneck rings to the eyelet at the end. Not until he had fixed a reel and passed a line through the rings did he put the lovely thing into my hand.

So light it was, so firm, so persuasive; such a thing alive – a sceptre. I could do no more than say 'Oo!' and again, 'Oo!'

'A thrill, ain't it?' said he.

I had no need to answer that. In my new-found rapture was only one sorrow – the knowledge that such happiness would not endure, and that, all too soon, a blank and rodless future awaited me.

'They must be awfully – awfully 'spensive,' I said.

'Couple of guineas,' he replied off-handedly.

A couple of guineas! And we were poor folk and the future was more rodless than ever.

'Then I shall save and save and save,' I said.

And my imagination started to add up twopence a week into guineas. Two hundred and forty pennies to the pound, multiplied by two – four hundred and eighty – and then another twenty-four pennies – five hundred and four. Why, it would take a lifetime, and no sweets, no elastic for catapults, no penny novelty boxes or air gun bullets or ices or anything.

Tragedy must have been writ large upon my face, for he said suddenly, 'When's your birthday?'

I was almost ashamed to tell him how soon it was. Perhaps he, too, was a little taken aback by its proximity, for that future uncle of mine was not so rich as uncles should be.

'We must see about it.'

'But it wouldn't – it couldn't be one like that,' I said.

I must have touched his pride, for he answered loftily, 'Certainly it will.'

In the fortnight that followed I walked on air and told everybody I had as 'good as got a couple-of-guineas rod'.

No one can deceive a child, save the child himself, and when my birthday came and with it a long brown paper parcel, I knew, even before I had removed the wrappers, that this two-guinea rod was not worth the money. There was a brown linen case, it is true, but it was not a case with a neat compartment for each joint, nor was there a spear in the flap. There was only one top instead of two, and there were no popping little stoppers to protect the ferrules from dust and injury. The lower joint boasted no elegant cork hand piece, but was a tapered affair coarsely made and rudely varnished.

When I fitted the pieces together, what I balanced in my hand was tough and stodgy rather than limber. The reel, which had come in a different parcel, was of wood. It had neither check nor brake, and the line overran and back-wound itself with distressing frequency.

I had not read and reread Garnages' price list without knowing something of rods, and I did not need to look long at this rod before realising that it was no match to the one I had handled on the Grayshott Road.

I believe at first a great sadness possessed me, but very presently imagination came to the rescue. For I told myself that I had only to think that this was the rod of all other rods that I desired most and it would be so. And it was so.

Furthermore, I told myself that, in this great wide, ignorant world, but few people existed with such expert knowledge of rods as I possessed. That I had but to say, 'Here is the final word in good rods,' and they would accept it as such.

Very confidently I tried the experiment on my mother, with inevitable success. From the depths of her affection and her ignorance on all such matters she produced:

'It's a magnificent rod.'

I went my way, knowing full well that she knew not what she said, but that she was kind.

With rather less confidence I approached my father, saying, 'Look, father! It cost two guineas. It's absolutely the best sort you can get.'

And he, after waggling it a few moments in silence, quoted cryptically:

'There is nothing either good or bad, but thinking makes it so.'

Young as I was, I had some curiosity about words, and on any other occasion I would have called on him to explain. But this I did not do, but left hurriedly, for fear that he should explain.

*

In the two years that followed, I fished every day in the slip of a back garden of our tiny London house. And, having regard to the fact that this rod was never fashioned to throw a fly, I acquired a pretty knack in the fullness of time and performed some glib casting at the nasturtiums and marigolds that flourished by the back wall.

My parents' fortunes must have been in the ascendant, I suppose, for I call to mind an unforgettable breakfast when my mother told me that father had decided we should spend our summer holiday at a Welsh hotel on the river Lledr. The place was called Pont-y-pant, and she showed me a picture of the hotel with a great knock-me-down river creaming past the front of it.

Although in my dreams I had heard fast water often enough, I had never seen it, and the knowledge that in a month's time I should wake with the music of a cataract in my ears was almost more than patience could endure.

In that exquisite, intolerable period of suspense I suffered as only childish longing and enthusiasm can suffer. Even the hank of gut that I bought and bent into innumerable casts failed to alleviate that suffering. I would walk for miles for a moment's delight captured in gluing my nose to the windows of tackleists' shops in the West End.

I learned from my grandmother – a wise and calm old lady – how to make nets and, having mastered the art, I made myself a landing net. This I set up on a frame fashioned from a penny schoolmaster's cane bound to an old walking stick. It would be pleasant to record that this was a good and serviceable net, but it was not. It flopped over in a very distressing fashion when called upon to lift the lightest weight. I had to confess to myself that I had more enthusiasm than skill in the manufacture of such articles.

At school there was a boy who had a fishing creel, which he swapped with me for a Swedish knife, a copy of *Rogues of the Fiery Cross*, and an Easter egg which I had kept on account of its rare beauty.

He had forced a hard bargain and was sure he had the best of it, but I knew otherwise.

At last the great day dawned, and after infinite travel by train we reached our destination as the glow of sunset was greying into dark. The river was in spate, and as we crossed a tall stone bridge on our way to the hotel I heard it below me, barking and grumbling among great rocks. I was pretty far gone in tiredness, for I remember little else that night but a rod rack in the hall – a dozen rods of different sorts and sizes, with gaudy salmon flies, some nets, a gaff, and an oak coffer upon which lay a freshly caught salmon on a blue ashet. Then supper by candlelight, bed, a glitter of stars through the open window, and the ceaseless drumming of water.

By six o'clock next morning I was on the river bank, fitting my rod together and watching in awe the great brown ribbon of water go fleetly by.

Among my most treasured possessions were half a dozen flies, and two of these I attached to the cast with exquisite care. While so engaged, a shadow fell on the grass beside me and, looking up, I beheld a lank, shabby individual with a walrus moustache and an unhealthy face, who, the night before, had helped with our luggage at the station.

'Water's too heavy for flies,' said he, with an uptilting inflection. 'This evening, yes; now, no – none whateffer. Better try with a worrum in the burrun.'

He pointed at a busy little brook which tumbled down the steep hillside and joined the main stream at the garden end.

'C-couldn't I fish with a fly in the – burrun?' I asked, for although I wanted to catch a fish very badly, for honour's sake I would fain take it on a fly.

'Indeed, no,' he replied, slanting the tone of his voice skyward. 'You cootn't. Neffer. And that isn't a fly rod whateffer.'

'It is,' I replied hotly. 'Yes, it is.'

But he only shook his head and repeated, 'No,' and took the rod from my hand and illustrated its awkwardness and handed it back with a wretched laugh.

If he had pitched me into the river I should have been happier.

'It is a fly rod and it cost two guineas,' I said, and my lower lip trembled.

'Neffer,' he repeated. 'Five shillings would be too much.'

Even a small boy is entitled to some dignity.

Picking up my basket, I turned without another word and made for the hotel. Perhaps my eyes were blinded with tears, for I was about to plunge into the dark hall when a great, rough, kindly voice arrested me with:

'Easy does it.'

At the thick end of an immense salmon rod there strode out into the sunlight the noblest figure I had ever seen.

There is no real need to describe my colonel again – I have done so already – but the temptation is too great. Standing in the doorway, the sixteen-foot rod in hand, the deerstalker hat, besprent with flies, crowning his shaggy head, the waders, like sevenleague boots, braced up to his armpits, the creel across his shoulder, a gaff across his back, he looked what he was – a god. His eyes met mine with that kind of smile one good man keeps for another.

'An early start,' he said. 'Any luck, old fellar?'

I told him I hadn't started – not yet.

'Wise chap,' said he. 'Water's a bit heavy for trouting. It'll soon run down through. Let's vet those flies of yours.'

He took my rod and whipped it expertly.

'A nice piece – new, eh?'

'N-not quite,' I stammered; 'but I haven't used it yet, sir, in water.'

That god read men's minds.

'I know – garden practice; capital; nothing like it.'

Releasing my cast, he frowned critically over the flies – a Blue Dun and a March Brown.

'Think so?' he queried. 'You don't think it's a shade late in the season for these fancies?' I said I thought perhaps it was. 'Yes, I think you're right,' said he. 'I believe in this big water you'd do better with a livelier pattern. Teal and Red, Cock-y-bundy, Greenwell's Glory.'

I said nothing, but nodded gravely at these brave names.

Once more he read my thoughts and saw through the wicker sides of my creel a great emptiness.

'I expect you've fished most in southern rivers. These Welsh trout have a fancy for a spot of colour.'

He rummaged in the pocket of his Norfolk jacket and produced a round tin which once had held saddle soap.

'Collar on to that,' said he; 'there's a proper pickle of flies and casts in that tin that, as a keen fisherman, you won't mind sorting out. Still, they may come in useful.'

'But, I say, you don't mean——' I began.

'Yes, go on; stick to it. All fishermen are members of the same club, and I'm giving the trout a rest for a bit.' His eyes ranged the hills and trees opposite. 'I must be getting on with it before the sun's too high.'

Waving his free hand, he strode away and presently was lost to view at a bend in the road.

I think my mother was a little piqued by my abstraction during breakfast. My eyes never for an instant deserted the round tin box which lay open beside my plate. Within it were a paradise and a hundred miracles all tangled together in the pleasantest disorder. My mother said something about a lovely walk over the hills, but I had other plans, which included a very glorious hour which should be spent untangling and wrapping up in neat squares of paper my new treasures.

'I suppose he knows best what he wants to do,' she said.

So it came about that I was left alone, and betook myself to a sheltered spot behind a rock where all the delicious disorder was remedied and I could take stock of what was mine.

I am sure there were at least six casts all set up with flies, and ever so many loose flies and one great stout, tapered cast, with a salmon fly upon it, that was so rich in splendour that I doubted if my benefactor could really have known that it was there.

I felt almost guilty at owning so much, and not until I had done full justice to everything did I fasten a new cast to my line and go a-fishing.

There is a lot said and written about beginner's luck, but none of it came my way. Indeed, I spent most of the morning extricating my line from the most fearsome tangles. I had no skill in throwing a cast with two droppers upon it and I found it was an art not to be learned in a minute.

Then, from overeagerness, I was too snappy with my back cast, whereby before many minutes had gone I heard that warning crack behind me that betokens the loss of a tail fly. I must have spent half an hour searching the meadow for that lost fly and finding it not. Which is not strange, for I wonder has any fisherman ever found that lost fly. The reeds, the buttercups, and the little people with many legs who run in the wet grass conspire together to keep the secret of its hiding place.

I gave up at last, and with a feeling of shame that was only proper, I invested a new fly on the point of my cast and set to work again, but more warily.

In that hard racing water a good strain was put upon my rod, and before the morning was out it was creaking at the joints in a way that kept my heart continually in my mouth. It is the duty of a rod to work with a single smooth action and by no means to divide its performance into three sections of activity. It is a hard task for any angler to persuade his line austerely if his rod behaves thus.

When, at last, my father strolled up the river bank, walking, to his shame, much nearer the water than a good fisherman should, my nerves were jumpy from apprehension.

'Come along. Food's ready. Done any good?' he said.

Again it was to his discredit that he put food before sport, but I told him I had had a wonderful morning, and he was glad.

'What do you want to do this afternoon, old man?' he asked.

'Fish,' I said.

'But you can't always fish,' he said.

I told him I could, and I was right, and have proved it for thirty years and more.

'Well, well,' he said, 'please yourself, but isn't it dull not catching anything?'

And I said, as I've said a thousand times since, 'As if it could be.'

So that afternoon I went downstream instead of up, and

found myself in difficult country where the river boiled between the narrows of two hills. Stunted oaks overhung the water and great boulders opposed its flow. Presently I came to a sort of natural flight of steps – a pool and a cascade three times repeated – and there, watching the maniac fury of the waters in awe and wonderment, I saw the most stirring sight in my young life.

I saw a silver salmon leap superbly from the cauldron below into the pool above. And I saw another and another salmon do likewise. And I wonder the eyes of me did not fall out of my head.

I cannot say how long I stayed watching that gallant pageant of leaping fish – in ecstasy there is no measurement of time – but at last it came upon me that all the salmon in the sea were careering past me and that if I were to realise my soul's desire I must hasten to the pool below before the last of them had gone by.

It was a mad adventure, for until I had discovered that stout cast, with the gaudy fly attached in the tin box, I had given no thought to such noble quarry. My recent possessions had put ideas into my head above my station and beyond my powers. Failure, however, means little to the young, and, walking fast, yet gingerly, for fear of of breaking my rod top against a tree, I followed the path downstream until I came to a great basin of water into which, through a narrow throat, the river thundered like a storm.

At the head of the pool was a plate of rock scored by the nails of fishermen's boots, and here I sat me down to wait while the salmon cast, removed from its wrapper, was allowed to soak and soften in a puddle left by the rain.

And while I waited a salmon rolled not ten yards from where I sat. Head and tail, up and down he went, a great monster of a fish, sporting and deriding me.

With that performance so near at hand, I have often wondered how I was able to control my fingers well enough to tie a figure-eight knot between the line and the cast. But I did, and I'm proud to be able to record it. Your true-born angler does not go blindly to work until he has first satisfied his conscience. There is a pride, in knots, of which the laity knows nothing, and if, through neglect to tie them rightly, failure and loss should result pride may not be restored nor conscience salved by the plea of eagerness.

With my trembling fingers I bent the knot, and with a pummelling heart, launched the line into the broken water at the throat of the pool.

At first the mere tug of the water against that large fly was so thrilling to me that it was hard to believe that I had not hooked a whale. The trembling line swung round in a wide arc into a calm eddy below where I stood. Before casting afresh I shot a glance over my shoulder to assure myself there was no limb of a tree behind me to foul the fly. And this was a gallant cast, true and straight, with a couple of yards more length than its predecessor, and a wide radius. Instinctively I knew, as if the surface had been marked with an × where the salmon had risen, that my fly must pass right over the spot. As it swung by, my nerves were strained like piano wires. I think I knew that something tremendous, impossible, terrifying was going to happen. The sense, the certitude was so strong in me that I half opened my mouth to shout a warning to the monster, not to.

I must have felt very, very young in that moment. I, who that same day had been talked to as a man by a man among men. The years were stripped from me and I was what I was – ten years old and appalled.

And then, with the suddenness of a rocket, it happened. The water was cut into a swathe. I remember a silver loop bearing downwards – a bright, shining, vanishing thing like the bobbin of my mother's sewing machine – and a tug. I shall never forget the viciousness of that tug. I had my fingers tight upon the line, so I got the full force of it. To counteract a tendency to go head first into the spinning water below, I threw myself backward and sat down on the hard rock with a jar that shut my teeth on my tongue – like the jaws of a trap.

Luckily I had let the rod go out straight with the line, else it must have snapped in the first frenzy of the down stream rush. Little ass that I was, I tried to check the speeding line with my forefinger, with the result that it cut and burnt me to the bone. There wasn't above twenty yards of line in the reel, and the wretched contrivance was trying to be rid of the line even faster than the fish was wrenching it out.

Heaven knows why it didn't snarl, for great loops and whorls were whirling, like Catherine wheels, under my wrist. An instant's glance revealed the terrifying fact that there were not more than half a dozen yards left on the reel, and the fish showed no sign of abating his rush. With the realisation of impending and inevitable catastrophe upon me, I launched a yell for help, which, rising above the roar of the waters, went echoing down the gorge.

And then, to add to my terrors, the salmon leaped – a swinging leap like a silver arch appearing and instantly disappearing upon the broken surface. So mighty, so all-powerful he seemed in that sublime moment that I lost all sense of reason and raised the rod, with a sudden jerk, above my head.

I have often wondered, had the rod actually been the two-guinea rod my imagination claimed for it, whether it could have withstood the strain thus violently and unreasonably imposed upon it. The wretched thing that I held so grimly never even put up a fight. It snapped at the ferrule of the lower joint and plunged like a toboggan down the slanting line, to vanish into the black depths of the water.

My horror at this calamity was so profound that I was lost even to the consciousness that the last of my line had run out. A couple of vicious tugs advised me of this awful truth. Then, snap! The line parted at the reel, flickered out through the rings, and was gone. I was left with nothing but the butt of a broken rod in my hand, and an agony of mind that even now I cannot recall without emotion.

I am not ashamed to confess that I cried. I lay down on the rock with my cheek in the puddle where I had soaked the cast, and plenished it with my tears. For what had the future left for me but a cut and burning finger, a badly bumped behind, the single joint of a broken rod, and no faith in uncles?

How long I lay there weeping I do not know. Ages, perhaps, or minutes, or seconds.

I was roused by a rough hand on my shoulder, and a kindly voice demanding, 'Hurt yourself, Ike Walton?'

Blinking away my tears, I pointed at my broken rod with a bleeding forefinger.

'Come! This is bad luck,' said my colonel, his face grave as a stone. 'How did it happen?'

'I c-caught a s-salmon.'

'You what?' he said.

'I d-did,' I said.

He looked at me long and earnestly; then, taking my injured hand, he looked at that and nodded.

'The poor groundlings who can find no better use for a river than something to put a bridge over think all fishermen are liars,' said he. 'But we know better, eh? By the bumps and breaks and cuts I'd say you made a plucky fight against heavy odds. Let's hear all about it.'

So, with his arm round my shoulders and his great shaggy head near to mine, I told him all about it.

At the end he gave me a mighty and comforting squeeze, and he said, 'The loss of one's first big fish is the heaviest loss I know. One feels, whatever happens, one'll never—' He stopped and pointed dramatically. 'There it goes – see! Down there at the tail of the pool!'

In the broken water where the pool emptied itself into the shallows beyond I saw the top joints of my rod dancing on the surface.

'Come on!' he shouted, and gripping my hand, jerked me to my feet. 'Scatter your legs! There's just a chance!'

Dragging me after him, we raced along by the river path to the end of the pool, where, on a narrow promontory of grass, his enormous salmon rod was lying.

'Now,' he said, picking it up and making the line whistle to and fro in the air with sublime authority, 'keep your eyes skinned on those shallows for another glimpse of it.'

A second later I was shouting, 'There! There!'

He must have seen the rod point at the same moment, for his line flowed out and the big fly hit the water with a plop not a couple of feet from the spot.

He let it ride on the current, playing it with a sensitive touch like the brushwork of an artist.

'Half a jiffy!' he exclaimed at last. 'Wait! Yes, I think so. Cut down to that rock and see if I haven't fished up the line.'

I needed no second invitation and presently was yelling, 'Yes – yes, you have!'

'Stretch yourself out then and collar hold of it.'

With the most exquisite care he navigated the line to where I lay stretched upon the rock. Then:

'Right you are! Good lad! I'm coming down.'

Considering his age, he leaped the rocks like a chamois.

'Now,' he said, and took the wet line delicately between his forefinger and thumb. One end trailed limply downstream, but the other end seemed anchored in the big pool where I had had my unequal and disastrous contest.

Looking into his face, I saw a sudden light of excitement dancing in his eyes.

'Odd,' he muttered, 'but not impossible.'

'What isn't?' I asked breathlessly.

'Well, it looks to me as if the top joints of that rod of yours have gone downstream.'

Gingerly he pulled up the line, and presently an end with a broken knot appeared.

'The reel knot, eh?' I nodded gloomily. 'Then we lose the rod,' said he. That wasn't very heartening news. 'On the other hand, it's just possible the fish is still on – sulking.'

'Oo!' I exclaimed.

'Now, steady does it,' he warned, 'and give me my rod.'

Taking a pair of clippers from his pocket, he cut his own line just above the cast.

'Can you tie a knot?' he asked.

'Yes,' I nodded.

'Come on then; bend your line on to mine. Quick as lightning.'

Under his critical eye I joined the two lines with a blood knot. 'I guessed you were a fisherman,' he said, nodded approvingly, and clipped off the ends. 'And now to know the best or the worst.'

I shall never forget the music of that check reel or the suspense with which I watched as, with the butt of the rod bearing against the hollow of his thigh, he steadily wound up the wet slack line. Every instant I expected it to come drifting downstream, but it didn't. Presently it rose in a tight slant from the pool above.

'Snagged, I'm afraid,' he said, and worked the rod with an easy straining motion to and fro. 'Yes, I'm afraid – no, by Lord Bobs, he's on!'

I think it was only right and proper that I should have launched a yell of triumph as, with the spoken word, the point at which the line cut the water shifted magically from the left side of the pool to the right.

'And a fish too,' said he.

In the fifteen minutes that followed, I must have experienced every known form of terror and delight.

'Youngster,' said he, 'you should be doing this by rights, but I'm afraid the rod's a bit above your weight.'

'Oh, go on and catch him,' I pleaded.

'And so I will,' he promised; 'unship the gaff, young un, and stand by to use it, and if you break the cast we'll never speak to each other again, and that's a bet.'

But I didn't break the cast. The noble, courageous, indomitable example of my river god had lent me skill and precision beyond my years. When at long last a weary, beaten, silver monster rolled within reach of my arm into a shallow eddy, the steel gaff shot out fair and true and sank home.

And then I was lying on the grass, with my arms round a salmon that weighed twenty-two pounds on the scale and contained every sort of happiness known to a boy.

And best of all, my river god shook hands with me and called me 'partner'.

That evening the salmon was placed upon the blue ashet in the hall, bearing a little card with its weight and my name upon it.

And I am afraid I sat on a chair facing it for ever so long, so that I could hear what the other anglers had to say as they passed by. I was sitting there when my colonel put his head out of his private sitting-room and beckoned me in.

'A true fisherman lives in the future, not the past, old man,' said he; 'though, for this once, it 'ud be a shame to reproach you.'

'We got the fish,' said he, 'but we lost the rod, and the future without a rod doesn't bear thinking of. Now' – and he pointed at a long wooden box on the floor, that overflowed with rods of different sorts and sizes – 'rummage among those. Take your time and see if you can find anything to suit you.'

'Oo, sir,' I said.

'Here, quit that,' he ordered gruffly. 'By Lord Bobs, if a show like this afternoon's don't deserve a medal, what does? Now, here's a handy piece by Hardy – a light and useful tool – or if you fancy greenheart in preference to split bamboo—'

I have the rod to this day, and I count it among my dearest treasures. And to this day I have a flick of the wrist that was his legacy. I have, too, some small skill in dressing flies, the elements of which were learned in his company by candlelight after the day's work was over. And I have countless memories of that month-long, month-short friendship – the closest and most perfect friendship, perhaps, of all my life.

He came to the station and saw me off.

How I vividly remember his shaggy head at the window, with the whiskered cheeks and the gunpowder marks at the corners of his eyes! I didn't cry, although I wanted to awfully. We were partners and shook hands. I never saw him again, although on my birthdays I would have coloured cards from him, with Irish, Scotch, Norwegian postmarks. Very brief they were: 'Water very low.' 'Took a good fish last Thursday.' 'Been prawning, but don't like it.'

Sometimes at Christmas I had gifts – a reel, a tapered line, a fly book. But I never saw him again.

Came at last no more postcards or gifts, but in the *Fishing Gazette*, of which I was a religious reader, was an obituary telling how one of the last of the Mutiny veterans had joined the great majority. It seems he had been fishing half an hour before he died.

So he was no more – my river god – and what was left to him they had put into a box and buried it in the earth.

But that isn't true; nor is it true that I never saw him again. For I seldom go a-fishing but that I meet him on the river banks.

The banks of a river are frequented by a strange company and are full of mysterious and murmurous sounds – the cluck and laughter of water, the piping of birds, the hum of insects, and the whispering of wind in the willows. What should prevent a man in such a place having a word and speech with another who is not there? So much of fishing lies in imagination, and mine needs little stretching to give my river god a living form.

'With this ripple,' says he, 'you should do well.'

'And what's it to be,' say I – 'Blue Upright, Red Spinner? What's your fancy, sir?'

Spirits never grow old. He has begun to take an interest in dry fly methods – that river god of mine, with his seven-league boots, his shaggy head, and the gaff across his back.

AN UNLIKELY HAUL

Lord Dunsany

AN UNLIKELY HAUL

There is a certain attitude taken by some at the Billiards Club towards my friend Jorkens, which I hope has not spread beyond its walls. If I were to express that attitude in a single word, the word would be Doubt. Whether any who have read some of the tales that I have recorded from time to time as I heard them from Jorkens may have felt any doubts of them I do not know, but I set down this tale not entirely for any slight interest it may possess for those interested in wells and the various objects their waters may be sometimes found to contain; but I more particularly record it because I know the tale to be true, being acquainted with one of the men to whom it occurred, and able thereby to check Jorkens' veracity, who was there as a chance onlooker, but a perfectly accurate one.

'I was taking a walk in India,' Jorkens began.

'What for?' asked Terbut.

'To get away from the flies,' said Jorkens.

'How far did you have to go to do that?' asked Terbut.

'Three thousand miles,' said Jorkens. 'But why not start? In fact I felt I couldn't delay any longer. Perhaps you don't know those flies?'

Terbut shook his head rather impatiently; for we all knew, and Jorkens better than most of us, that Terbut had never travelled.

'Well,' Jorkens continued, 'I was walking over a plain with a good deal of grass on it, and it was hot enough to kill more than grass, and there was nothing to see on it except a horse grazing, if nibbling that withered stuff can be so described; and he was grazing with a bit in his mouth and a saddle on his back. And then I came suddenly on a well. A rather thick patch of grass hid it entirely, until I was right on top of it.

And when I did get there I saw a little flight of steps, cut out of the dry mud of which all that part of the world seems to be made, going down to the well. And on one of the lower steps a man was seated, holding a rod. I never saw him till I stood at the top step, and he didn't see me even then, being so intent on the water.

' "Fishing?" ' I said.

' "It's a spear," ' he answered, and sat there patiently for a few more seconds, leaning over the water not looking at me, then made a jab. There was some commotion in the well, in fact more noise than I ever heard in any well before, and then he made another jab; and this time, above the noise of the threshing of water, I clearly heard a pig squeal.

' "Have you got a pig in the well?" ' I asked.

' "Sounds like it," ' he said.

When the pig stopped squealing he leaned forward and began to pull; and very soon he hauled up a man out of the well, but the noise of some big thing swimming did not stop. It turned out from their conversation to each other, though they said little enough to me, that the second man had been hanging by one arm from the lower step of the well, the other arm being broken. The noise in the well continued, and rather puzzled me.

' "Have you got anything more down there?" ' I asked them.

' "Only a horse," ' said the one that I had mistaken for a fisherman. And he went on with his angling, until he got a pair of reins on the end of his spear. And sure enough there was a horse at the end of the reins, just as the man had said. I admit I hadn't believed him all at once, and perhaps it is rather a lesson to us not to disbelieve a thing merely because it's unlikely; and a horse in a well seemed so very unlikely, especially a well that already had so much else in it. But I was wrong, for very soon I saw a horse's head appearing; and more than that the two men could not manage to bring to sight for a long time.'

'But what was it all about?' asked Terbut. 'What were they doing?'

'They told me that,' said Jorkens. 'They were a long while getting the horse out, and every now and then one of them would call out to me a few words of explanation: you couldn't call it a story, just explanation. And what I gathered from it all was that they had been out pig-sticking and they had come on a lot of pigs, a sounder they call them, rustling in the long grass where they could not see them. And they had ridden up to a little village and got some men to go into the grass making noises, and some of the natives had brought their dogs with them; and all the pigs had come out and they had ridden after the biggest. They got right away from the long grass at once and saw no more of it, except little patches that they scarcely noticed; in fact the one beside which we all met they never noticed at all, nor did the pig; or, if he did, he went straight for it because it reminded him of home; nor did the first horse, nor his rider. And they all went into the well.

'The pig climbed on to the horse's back, to keep himself out of the water; and the horse kept on rolling sideways as he swam, so as to put the pig back in the well. And that is another unusual thing to see, I mean a pig riding a horse; but, again, one should not disbelieve it merely on that account. I don't claim to have seen it myself, but the man who killed the pig saw it; in fact he killed it actually in the saddle. He killed the pig first because it seemed to make more room in the well, especially considering how near his tusks kept coming to the shoulder-blades of the man who was hanging by one arm from the bottom step. And then he pulled the man out. Getting the horse out was the hardest job of the lot.'

'Did you lend them a hand with the horse?' asked Terbut, rather unnecessarily.

'Well, no,' said Jorkens, 'I was perfectly ready to, but the fellow took offence at a quite natural remark that I made in all innocence. It was a simple and harmless remark, and very much to the point. But he took offence at it.'

'What did you say to him?' I asked.

'I merely said,' replied Jorkens, ' "Nice for their drinking water." '

TROUTMANSHIP

Stephen Potter

TROUTMANSHIP

What a complex world is here! Yet in the relatively small province of our little correspondence college we have made enormous headway and gained the thanks of all the fishership community by defining once and for all the two basic trout approaches, in one of which students are expected to satisfy the examiners.

Our decontamination reader in Trout, J. Hargreaves, is a pleasant teacher who plays the two-approach system admirably himself. With newcomers, he demonstrates this twoness with a pair of ordinary fishing rods, one of which is new, the other old.

Rodmanship

This basic gambit is, basically, the art of being one-up with one's rod. Most commonly, the man who still keeps his old rod is pitted against the man who has just bought a new one. Old Rod makes first move:

OLD ROD *(looking at New Rod's new rod)*: I like it. I like it. I like it. Of course I'm in my forties. I suppose my old one will see me through. Ought to. Ought to. Ought to.

NEW ROD *(countering implied criticism)*: I was sorry to see my last rod go. . . . But if one really *fishes* in water like this . . . you know . . . I suppose one kills about a rod a season? Mind you, if you don't go in for these acrobatic casts I'm always attempting rather unsuccessfully . . .

OLD ROD *(pretending to suspect origin of rod and holding it in his hand)*: Tell me – where did you . . . *(our inflection for 'where did you' can imply not only that rod was mass produced, but stamped out of synthetic wood.)*

NEW ROD: Well – you know – 'Jackie' Bampton happens to be rather a friend of mine. And my difficulty is that I'm not really comfy unless the action is, well, inches nearer the butt than normal—

OLD ROD *(out-gambited but fighting back)*: Don't worry . . . don't worry . . . it's like a woman. You get used to it. In a couple of years, anyhow, it will be part of you. Even if you don't catch any trout.

If New Rod's rod is longer, with a longer line, and if the river needs such a rod, Old Rod will be in difficulty. Spandrel's Underthwart can be used here.

SPANDREL *(old rodding)*: Nice rod, but it isn't alive till you're about fifteen yards out. I like to throw a shorter line myself.

With right inflection, O.R. can suggest that he is an ancient, almost neolithic, virtuoso of the trout-stream, a sort of Red Indian, really, belly to the ground, who finds no difficulty in trout work at ten yards.[1]

Troutmanship Basic

After practice in the two-approach system with rods, students may then start practising troutmanship proper.

This, too, is essentially an A *vs.* B situation. A the purist, the scholar of dry fly, *vs.* B the rough and ready, the ham, the hack.

Tell my frankly, says A the purist, *were you fishing the water or the rise?*

To counter this accusation of just chucking about, the

student trained in Old Rodship should have no difficulty. I'm bound to say that Gattling-Fenn was at his best in this situation. Shirt open to the waist and apparently nut-brown to the navel (actually he wore a 'Suntan Gypsyvest'), Gattling was able to imply 'for Heaven's sake.'

'For Heaven's sake,' he said, and the gleam of his almost suspiciously white teeth suggested 'I'm just a hobo, son – a tramp. My father, and his father before him,[2] were born natural hunters to a man, like every Englishman born a mother's son.'

While suggesting every word of this, Gattling was at the same time able actually to say:

'I had him in a corner – and – yes, I'm bound to say the fly was a bit damp! Spam Special. Yes, I had to rob the sandwich. . . .'

The following Hargreaves Hampers are worth study, and are useful to others besides troutmen.

1. Do not cast in presence of other fishermen. Proved odds are 93 to 1 against anything happening. So if A says: 'Have a go at him,' you, B, should reply either: 'No – you. I had a good day yesterday,' *or:* 'Oh, that one? He's nearly had me once already. Ruddy great chub.'

2. For use against man who catches fish bigger than yours in same water.

TROUTMAN: That's a good one. What does it weigh?

LAYMAN (*cool*): I don't carry scales.

TROUTMAN: I'll weigh it for you . . . 1 3/4 pounds. That's funny. How long is it?

LAYMAN Frankly, I don't carry a tape measure either.

TROUTMAN: I do. . . . Thought so. Nearly 16 inches. That's the trouble with this water, it won't stand fish this size. Ought to be two pounds. It's gone back.

Layman begins to realise he has caught a fish almost on its knees and practically fainting for want of food. He could have picked it out of the water with his bare hands.

3. Rub it in. If, for instance, rival makes clumsy cast, go on and on pointing it out. Thus:

TROUTMAN (*smiling through clenched teeth*): *Now* you've put him down. Now you *have* put him down. Crikey, were you trying to brain him? Doubt if he'll put his nose up for a week. Should think he'd rather drown. I'll move upstream a bit, I think. Happens to all of us.

Marshall's Mangier

This subject is still very 'young' as we call it at Yeovil – i.e. there is still a lot of loose fishing play within our orbit, and a dozen gambits not yet properly described. That is why I am glad to mention Marshall's 'Mangler' – a gambit invented by H. Marshall and needing a finesse and urbanity of execution which totally belie its sobriquet.

The general object is to express an enormous Upper

Sixthism so devastating that practically no one else can ever speak about fishing again; and it is done in this way.

The catching of your specific fish is *a Problem*, and must be so approached, without fervour, without even enjoyment.

On one side of your equation is your possible fly, *x*: on the other, certain variables.

Let α = weather forecast.
 γ = weather.
 γ^i = flow of stream in relation to mean number of solid factory deposits and old cans.
 β = probable age of trout.
 o = probable age of fisherman.
 π = distance of nearest active motor-bicycle or farm tractor.
 δ = temperature of fish.

Then, by a simple calculation jotted down in a waterproof tent with unrunnable ink on unsmudgeable paper, Marshall would get some such equation as this:

$$x = \frac{\delta^{16}\,o\,\sqrt{\alpha^3\gamma}\ \gamma^i - 8}{\beta^2\,\pi} = \quad \text{Split's Indefatigable } or \text{ Aunt Mary's Special}$$

Hand this result with your rod to the ghillie and walk quite slowly away, leaving him to catch the actual fish. Marshall has learnt to intensify the effect of all this by turning up on the bank in a bowler hat and a dark pin-stripe and a pair of thin, blindingly well-polished black shoes, in which he delicately picks his way back through pool and undergrowth.

[1] Rodmanship Advance. This year has seen New Rod placed in the one down position by Newer Rod Still. This instrument is made of molecularly reconstituted toilet soap. And though it is associated with wrong-clothesmanship (jacket and trousers clean, and matching) and wrong gadgetmanship (fly-boxes made of perspex) the thing works. We are struggling with this embryonic counter:

NEWER ROD STILL: Yes, it's the first time these fish on the far side of the bend have had a fly decently presented to them.

COUNTERER: Well, I'm bound to admit it makes fishing easier.

N.R.S.: It certainly does.

COUNTERER: I mean, you *could* use a Mills bomb, I suppose.

[2] This would be Gattling-Fenn's grandfather.

CHRISTOPHER NORTH

John Wilson – who wrote, mainly for *Blackwood's Edinburgh Magazine*, under the pseudonym 'Christopher North' – was born in Paisley, Scotland in 1785. He entered the University of Glasgow aged just twelve, and Magdalen College, Oxford six years later. After graduating with a first class degree, he spent much of his twenties at his estate, Elleray, in Cumbria. He became well-acquainted with literary personalities such as William Wordsworth, Samuel Taylor Coleridge and Thomas de Quincey.

In 1811, North lost most of his fortune due to the dishonest speculation of an uncle, and had to move in with his mother in Edinburgh. He read law, and in 1816 produced a volume of poems, *The City of the Plague*. Shortly afterwards, he became the principal writer for the Tory monthly *Blackwood's Edinburgh Magazine*, where he was the chief composer of the hugely popular *Nodes Ambrosianae* series. In 1820, North was elected to the chair of Moral Philosophy at the University of Edinburgh, produced most of his best and best-known work for *Blackwood's* in the decade between 1825 and 1835. North died in 1854, aged 68.

JEROME K. JEROME

Jerome Klapka Jerome was born in Walsall, England in 1859. Both his parents died while he was in his early teens, and he was forced to quit school to support himself. Jerome worked for a number of years collecting coal along railway tracks, before trying his hand at acting, journalism, teaching and soliciting. At long last, in 1885, he had some success with *On the Stage – and Off*, a comic memoir of his experiences with an acting troupe. Jerome produced a number of essays over the following years, and married in 1888, spending the honeymoon in "a little boat" on the Thames.

In 1889, Jerome published his most successful and best-remembered work, *Three Men in a Boat*. Featuring himself and two of his friends encountering humorous situations while floating down the Thames in a small boat, the book was an instant success, and has never been out of print. In fact, its popularity was such that the number of registered Thames boats went up fifty percent in the year following its publication. With the financial security provided by *Three Men in a Boat*, Jerome was able to dedicate himself fully to writing, producing eleven more novels and a number of anthologies of short fiction.

In 1926, Jerome published his autobiography, *My Life and Times*. He died a year later, aged 68.

LORD DUNSANY

Lord Dunsany was born Edward John Moreton Drax Plunkett in London in 1878. Dunsany's youth was spent in Dunsany, Ireland – his family home – and Kent. He attended school at Cheam and Eton, before entering the Royal Military Academy Sandhurst in 1896. He inherited his father's title shortly before fighting in the Second Anglo-Boer War between 1899 and 1901. Dunsany published his first book a collection of Anglo-Irish fantasy stories entitled *The Gods of Pegana*, in 1905.

Over the course of his life, Dunsany was a prolific writer, penning short stories, novels, plays, poetry, essays and autobiography. During the peak of his career he was something of a literary celebrity, spending time with authors such as W. B. Yeats and Rudyard Kipling. He published over sixty books, and his plays were highly successful; at one point, five Dunsany works were running simultaneously in New York. His most notable fantasy short stories were published between 1905 and 1919, in collections such as *The Sword of Welleran and Other Stories* (1908), *A Dreamer's Tales* (1910), *The Book of Wonder* (1912) and *Tales of Wonder* (1916). Amongst his best-regarded novels are *Don Rodriguez: Chronicles of Shadow Valley* (1922), *The King of Elfland's Daughter* (1924), and *The Charwoman's Shadow* (1926).

Dunsany died in old age, following an attack of appendicitis. Over the course of his writing life, he greatly influenced a wide range of authors. Arthur C. Clarke called him "one of the greatest writers of [the 20th] century," and H. P. Lovecraft described him as being "unexcelled in the sorcery of crystalline singing prose, and supreme in the creation of a gorgeous and languorous world of incandescently exotic vision."

NEIL MUNRO

Neil Munro was born in Inveraray, Scotland in 1863. He spent much of his early life working in journalism, before turning to fiction writing, publishing a number of historical novels. Most of these featured a Highland setting; the best is generally considered to be *The New Road* (1914), set in 1733. Munro is arguably best-remembered in contemporary times, however, for his humours short stories, originally written under the pen name Hugh Foulis. A number of these featured the fictional steamboat the *Vital Spark* and her captain Para Handy. Munro died in 1930, aged 67. Although he has been somewhat forgotten since his death, in his day Munro was a hugely popular author; his obituaries described him as the successor of Robert Louis Stevenson, and the greatest Scottish novelist since Sir Walter Scott.

ROLAND PERTWEE

Roland Pertwee was born in Brighton, England in 1885. Pertwee served in the Army during the First World War, before retiring to pursue a career in the flourishing British film industry. Between the 1910s and the 1950s, Pertwee worked as a writer on an array of films, including MGM's *A Yank at Oxford*, alongside F. Scott Fitzgerald. He also tried his hand at acting in as many as ten different productions. In 1954, along with his older son, Michael, Pertwee created *The Grove Family*, widely regarded as the first soap opera in the history of British television. At its height, *The Grove Family* is said to have been watched by in one in every four television owners in the country. Pertwee produced a number of works of juvenile fiction, but it was his two short stories, 'The River God' and 'Fish Are Such Liars', that earned him major critical acclaim. Both pieces are now considered classics of the short form, and were published posthumously, in 1970.